MORE CREATIVE
GROWTH GAMES

MORE CREATIVE GROWTH GAMES

Eugene Raudsepp

A PERIGEE BOOK

Perigee Books
are published by
G.P. Putnam's Sons
200 Madison Avenue
New York, New York 10016

Library of Congress Cataloging in Publication Data

Raudsepp, Eugene.
   More creative growth games.

   (A Perigee book)
   1. Creative thinking—Problems, exercises, etc.
I. Title.
BF408.R243   153.3'5   79-20537
ISBN 0-399-50456-7

First Perigee Printing, 1980
Designed by Bernard Schleifer

Printed in the United States of America

CONTENTS

PART II: EXAMPLES AND ANSWERS

**PART III: A NEW LOOK AT
THE CREATIVE PROCESS**

ACKNOWLEDGMENTS

MANY INDIVIDUALS WHO LABOR in this fascinating vineyard of creativity have provided the inspiration and stimulus for various games and exercises in this book. Of particular usefulness have been the researches and conceptions of J. P. Guilford, Alex F. Osborn, Sidney J. Parnes, Sidney X. Shore, Silvan S. Tomkins, Edward de Bono, John E. Arnold, Ross L. Mooney, George M. Prince, and William J. J. Gordon.

Grateful acknowledgment is made to the following for permission to quote selections and exercises from their works: to Michael F. Andrews for *Pine Cone: Sensory Awareness Module,* © 1976 by Michael Andrews; for items appearing in "Sightwords" and "Thumbprint Cartoons" from *Creativity and Imagination,* by Jacolyn A. Mott, © 1973 Creative Educational Society, Inc.; for items in "Killer Phrases" to Charles H. Clark, president of Yankee Ingenuity Programs, Kent, Ohio; for "Empty Bottle Binge" to Fred C. Finsterbach, president of Educare Associates, Rome, N.Y.; for "What's Good About It?" "More Than Meets The Eye," and "Making Opportunities," from July 1973, March 1975, and March 1976 issues of *Creativity in Action* (newsletter), © Sidney X. Shore, publisher of *Creativity in Action,* Sharon, Connecticut; and to *Games* Magazine for Wacky Wordies, reprinted from *Games* Magazine (515 Madison Avenue, N.Y., N.Y. 10022). Copyright © 1979 by Playboy.

I also want to thank the following persons who helped me to test out some of the games and exercises: Ray and MaryAnn Wills, Charles and Annis Young, William L. Cesario, Andre DeZanger, Conor McMahon, and John Demarest. I am particularly indebted to my friend and colleague Joseph C. Yeager for many stimulating discussions and suggestions regarding the book. And finally, I want to express my appreciation to my daughters Kira and Zenia for their devotion and diligent help in typing the manuscript and for providing some of the illustrations.

MORE CREATIVE GROWTH GAMES

INTRODUCTION

WELCOME AGAIN to the world of creative growth! Readers from all over the world have written and called to express their delight at having experienced the games and exercises in *Creative Growth Games*. Many claim that the book helped them to substantially increase their creative capacities and to discover their submerged and neglected strengths and unique talents. Their exceedingly positive experience and response are responsible for spawning this sequel.

While working on this book, I started reflecting more and more on why creativity seems to be so basic for human happiness. It appears, indeed, that the final good and basic enjoyment of life lies in exercising one's creative capacities to become fully functioning and fully liberated. In this sense, happiness is synonymous with creative growth, and the opening up of new and rich potentialities for life that this growth makes possible. There exists in most human beings an unquenchable appetite for fruitful activity and for reaching ever higher levels of creative vitality.

Reflecting on the contemporary scene of rapid problems-escalation and complex changes, it again becomes obvious that increased creativity offers the only real hope for pro-active adaptation and, perhaps, even survival. The pivotal role which creativity plays seems to be important at three levels: civilization, organizations, and individuals.

Creativity and Civilization

Creativity is the mainspring of our civilization: from the concept of the wheel, through the steamboat, the spinning jenny, the telephone, the automobile, the airplane, and the radio to television, automation, the electronics industry, nuclear power, and space travel. All the milestones of great inventions, scientific discoveries and technological breakthroughs, as well as great painting, litera-

1

ture, music, drama, sculpture, and other forms of artistic expression have depended on creative thinking of the highest order. Thus, the progress of civilization and humanity's present evolutionary stature are essentially due to creativity and innovation. Were it not for man's inherent creative thrust for achievement, pitted perennially against insuperable odds, we would still be playfully swinging from limb to limb, stopping occasionally to diet on raw fruit and vegetables.

Creativity in Business and Industry

The tremendous importance of creativity and innovation has been clearly demonstrated in business and industry. In analyzing the dynamics of past growth and in developing long-range plans for the future, more perceptive managements have made some revealing discoveries about the role that creativity has played in corporate success. Some corporations have estimated that as much as 80 percent of their sales volume comes from products unknown to the market a decade ago. And even more impressive is the fact that more than 40 percent of the Gross National Product has been attributed to research and development within the past fifteen years.

Almost any modern business requires a continuous, unceasing input of new, practical, and usable ideas to stay viable and prosperous. New ideas are needed to increase efficiency in operations and procedures, to create more economical and effective ways of doing things, to tackle intractably stubborn and costly problems. New ideas are needed to develop new products and processes, to develop effective marketing strategies and sales campaigns, to respond to ever new challenges, problems, and issues in an innovative way. Indeed, just to survive, a corporation must produce a continuous flow of new products and processes. One marketing specialist has made the conservative prediction that any company that fails to introduce at least one *completely* or *radically* new product within the next five years will be hard put to stay in business.

Creativity plays a fundamental role in thinking, problem solving, and decision making in almost all corporate functions. It is so basic that it can, or should, be used in management, planning, communications, marketing, advertising, sales, public relations, finance, labor relations, employee relations, recruiting, operations

2

research, design, and other areas. As experience has shown, creative problem-solving techniques can be applied to any and all difficult decision situations.

What Makes a Creative Organization?

What do successful, creative organizations have in common? Their one common denominator is that the tried, the proven, and the established do not have an inordinately strong hold on them.

Creative, progressive organizations are ever alert to try new techniques and methods. They are ready to undertake pilot ventures and projects. They are hospitable to new ideas and pioneering concepts which because of their experimental nature do not find ready acceptance among the overly cautious organizations or among those where security is derived from the already consolidated success. Creative, dynamic organizations feel that they can afford to take chances, make leaps into the unknown, and venture occasionally into pioneering quicksand. They know that such action, even at the risk of many dry wells in the beginning, frequently delivers a real gusher in the end.

There is a theory that organizations follow the pattern of the human organism: birth, growth, development, plateau, slow decline and, finally, demise. This, however, need not be so. In organizations where creativity is continually and consciously encouraged and fostered, where the "climate" releases rather than inhibits creativity, the conditions that ensure continuous renewal and progress are clearly present.

Creativity and Accelerating Change

Creativity is most valuable in good times; it is mandatory in times of rapid change, increasing complexity, shifting goals, and new objectives. Creativity has now become everyone's business; it is no longer the exclusive province of the chosen few. As creativity-training courses have abundantly proven, creative problem-solving can be learned as a skill and then used deliberately to bring about useful and dynamic results.

Progressive organizations now recognize that we are squarely in the confrontation path of accelerating change. They also realize that to cope with complex, unprecedented problems and issues—even crises—generated by political events, modern technologies, socioeconomic changes, and new attitudes and values, people need more than ever the ability to think creatively. But creativity is not only the process of coping with change, it is one of the most useful tools to bring about constructive modifications—a course that will determine the future success of any organization. In an enlightened organizational setup, it occupies the center stage.

With each passing day it is becoming more and more apparent that creative adaptation and flexibility represent the only viable alternatives to failure or stagnation. Educator David Mars put it well when he said, "Organizations which are creative and adaptive can view the future with the confidence that they will be able to cope with it; organizations which are not creative and adaptive will probably not see the changes coming in the first place, and when these changes arrive, will be overwhelmed by the stresses which they will create."

Creativity and Education

Of the myriad problems we face, one of the most crucial to creativity is education. Much has been said and written about the shortcoming of educational systems that stifle creative impulse and have to a large degree contributed to the widespread disaffection and the creation of countercultures among our youth. All too often education has been viewed as an aggregation of facts or the preparatory stages for a conventional life. Creativity and invention is stifled in millions of school children and many have not gotten beyond rote learning.

Several striking experiments in recent years have demonstrated that learning is much more effective when it is done creatively. Instead of teaching and learning by authority, which is still the unquestioningly accepted method in most of our educational institutions, it would be more effective to adopt creative ways of teaching. This would provide encouragement and motivation for students to imagine, question, probe, explore, experiment, and test. Only then could we be sure that we are preparing the ever-renewing men and women, the doers and innovators our society so desperately needs.

The very rapid changes of our present age require that problems be tackled innovatively. It is estimated that the technological advancements and discoveries during the next couple of decades will surpass all the past accomplishments in human history. It is difficult to foretell exactly what knowledge will be needed to tackle future problems. What the young are learning now will surely become obsolete. Everyone can and must continue learning throughout his or her lifetime, but knowledge alone is no quarantee that we will meet future problems effectively. Only a cultivated creative ability provides the means necessary for coping with the ever-increasing complexity of future dilemmas.

Does specific training in creative problem-solving really make any difference in the development of creativity? The answer is a resounding "Yes." This is indicated by student reactions after completion of courses and workshops in creativity. Here is a sampling of reactions given by students in Buffalo State University College:

"I never knew how many problems I had. When you feel you can find answers, it is easier to admit you have problems."

"I feel I have found myself; everything is more optimistic. I want to create my life. I have discovered parts of me that I never knew existed."

"My understanding of the material in other courses has benefited because I've learned to probe deeper than I had before. I find myself always asking, 'why?' Or, 'How might I better my situation?' Before, I took things for granted and never took the time to question any further. Now I've found that there's a lot to be said about questioning."

"I learned to learn."

"This course has helped me not to be afraid to voice my opinions or how I feel about things."

Creativity and the Individual

Beyond the needs of society, another significant development in the present creativity movement is the recognition of its importance to an individual's psychological health. Instead of the long-standing concept that creative talent is the province of only a select few, it has now been discovered that most men and women possess a good deal of creative capacity, although it may be buried under layers and layers of personal and environmental barriers. We now recognize that there are degrees of creative capacity rather than a sharp cleavage between the creative and the less creative. As a result, there has been an upsurge of interest in releasing, developing, expanding, and stimulating each and everyone's creative powers. A momentum is gaining aimed at unfolding and developing each individual's creative ability, as dim as the spark may be, and kindling it to whatever flame it may conceivably develop.

There is a very personal significance to creativity; it is one of the most important outlets of personal expression, and is self-fulfilling and subjectively rewarding. Creativity is a crucial quality for a full and rich personality, and it contributes to a comprehensively healthy life.

Painter Stanley A. Czurles feels that the modern person has contracted the stifling malaise of "spectatoritis," which leads to increased feelings of sterility, lack of satisfaction, and apathy. In his view, only the creative person can experience true fulfillment in life. Czurles presents the following comparison of the two contrasting orientations and their effect on psychological health, attitudes toward life, and activities:

Spectator	*Creative Doer*
Kills time	Uses time to develop self
Is an observer	Is involved, experiences personal achievement
Has few self-sufficiency interests	Is rich in self-enriching activities
Seeks to have something happen to or for him	Is self-stimulating; is at home and in control of many conditions
Is involved in a merry-go-round of prestructured activities	Enjoys selected relevant activities
Has only temporary enjoyment, with little or no lasting product	Experiences continuous satisfaction, achieves tangible results, and becomes a more efficiently functioning person
Is swept into activities	Selects planned participation
Has fractionated experiences	Has completeness and continuity of involvement
Is prone to boredom	Is stimulated by challenging interests

Experiences no deep challenge	Aspires more as he or she achieves new goals
Accomplishes nothing very distinguishing	Grows in potential through unique achievements
Achieves shallow success	Acquires deeper meanings and new possibilities
Curtails himself or herself by a focus on pessimistic personal concerns	Is enlivened by a recognized freedom to pursue creative interests
Has increased hardening of opinions and attitudes	Continues being flexible through continuous new insights
Achieves superficial trappings of culture	Experiences the essence of a culture
Is subject to early spiritual-mental aging	Enjoys an extended youthful spirit
Experiences primarily what is	Experiences what might be

Both creativity and psychological health can be described in terms that belong to the same family of meanings. They are both associated with integration, wholeness, commitment, self-fulfillment, honesty, goal direction, vitality, enthusiasm, personal involvement, deeper self-realization, high motivation, greater self-knowledge, and action.

Our Present Concern with Creativity

Although creativity is one of the most valuable qualities of the human mind, interest in and systematic study of creativity are relatively recent phenomena. What accounts for the recent widespread interest in creativity and what does it signify? Some authorities believe it represents one of the most vital turning points for the better, away from the recent, rather awesome and disturbing trends in the world. Harold H. Anderson of Michigan State University says that although creativity is old, "what is new in creativity is the growing realization, the emerging discovery, of the tremendous unsuspected potentialities in the creativity of man, in the nature of human resources, in the meaning of respect for the individual. Such a discovery . . . may prove as significant as Darwinian evolution or atomic energy."

There are several notable people who maintain that our current intense interest in creativity—how to find it, how to nurture it and bring it to full flower—stems from the present dearth of significant creativity, the rapid changes in almost every realm of life, and the increasing number of complex and frustrating problems that have come to characterize our here-and-now. One of the most eloquent statements reflecting this thought belongs to psychologist Carl R. Rogers:

"I maintain that there is a desperate social need for the creative behavior of creative individuals. . . . Many of the serious criticisms of our culture and its trends may best be formulated in terms of a dearth of creativity. Let us state some of these very briefly: In education we tend to turn out conformists, stereotypes, individuals whose education is 'completed,' rather than freely creative and original thinkers.

"In our leisure-time activities, passive entertainment and regimented group action are overwhelmingly predominant, whereas creative activities are much less in evidence. In the sciences, there is an ample supply of technicians, but the number who can creatively formulate fruitful hypotheses and theories is small indeed. In industry, creation is reserved for the few—the manager, the designer, the head of the research department—whereas for the many life is devoid of original or creative endeavour.

"In a time when knowledge, constructive and destructive, is advancing by the most incredible leaps and bounds into a fantastic atomic age, genuinely creative adaptation seems to represent the only possibility that man can keep abreast of the kaleidoscopic change in his world."

This urgency for more creativity has been echoed by others. For example, educator Viktor Lowenfeld states, "In an age of increasing juvenile delinquency and mental illness, in an age where man seems threatened with self-extermination because of the wonderful forces his mind has unleashed, we must find ways to use this mindpower creatively—to build rather than to destroy. And we have no time to lose."

More Creative Growth Games

The present volume offers you an enjoyable and effective way to stimulate your creative capacities to levels you probably wouldn't have imagined possible. The games and exercises are education, entertainment, excitement, fun—powerful instruments for magnifying and accelerating your mental processes. In addition to your own creative self-development, they are ideal for group learning and sharing. They can be played alone or in a group of two or more.

More Creative Growth Games consists of more than 75 stimulating games and exercises designed to develop:

creative imagination	humor and wit
visualization and imagery	creative observation
originality	persistence
ingenuity	sensitivity to problems
flexibility	generation of viewpoints
fluency of thinking	intuitive thinking
and expression	transformation techniques
cluency	creative strategies
creative analysis and planning	synthesizing ability, and many
resourcefulness	other vital attributes of creative
creative empathy	thinking and problem solving
discernment	
metaphoric thinking	

Carefully designed and tested, they are aimed at helping you discover and strengthen new creative capacities . . . new inner experiences . . . new ways of imagining, perceiving, thinking, visualizing, and feeling. In addition, there is a concluding chapter explaining the important aspects of the process of creative thinking. Part II, the Answers and Examples section, provides you with copious examples to the games and exercises, as well as additional explanations of their practical usefulness.

Using your imagination is very enjoyable and stimulating, and you will find *More Creative Growth Games* challenging and fun to play. Each game and exercise is designed to give you understandings of new ways of thinking and perceiving, so you can develop, release, and expand every facet of your latent creative powers. The games and exercises range in difficulty from the (deceptively) simple, through moderate, to very challenging and difficult. Since the purpose of the book is not to test you, but provide you with an enjoyable and challenging learning experience, don't feel bad if your attempts at some of them are not immediately successful.

Will these games and exercises do the job? The games in this book—tried on hundreds of men and women—have conclusively proven that most individuals are able to increase their creative performance by 40 to over 300 percent.

I hope that the growth you will derive from *More Creative Growth Games* and the stimulus it provides your mind will surpass any other pursuit or training in which you might soon engage.

EUGENE RAUDSEPP
President
Princeton Creative Research, Inc.
Princeton, New Jersey

PART I

Games and Exercises

There are certain things that our age needs. It
needs, above all, courageous hope and the
impulse to creativeness.
—BERTRAND RUSSELL

What feeling, knowledge, or will man has
depends on the last resort upon what imagination
he has.
—SÖREN KIERKEGAARD

Man is happiest when he is creating. In fact, the
highest state of which man is capable lies in the
creative act.
—LEO BUSCAGLIA

The best way to escape from a problem is to
solve it.
—BRENDAN FRANCIS

I shall never respect my brains until I pick a few
gold coins from them.
—THOMAS WOLFE

Dive into the sea of thought, and find there
pearls beyond price.
—ABRAHAM IBN-EZRA

#1: HAVE A BALL!

If one were to pick two attributes most vital for creative problem-solving and for coping with the rapid change-dynamics of our time, these would be *fluency* and *flexibility*.

The creative person is both fluent and flexible. Capable of producing ideas in volume, he or she has a better chance of developing significant alternatives when confronting a problem or when seeking improvements in existing situations. The creative person is able to choose and investigate a wide variety of approaches to solve his problems. He is resourceful in the ability to shift gears, to discard one frame of reference for another, to change approaches and to adapt quickly to new developments. He constantly asks himself, "What else?" or "What would happen if I viewed my problem from a different perspective?"

This exercise is designed to enhance your facility to think up a large number of different ideas when confronting a problem. It can be done solo or in a group. A group usually generates a lot of excitement and a blizzard of ideas. When playing this game with others, agree to a 4-minute time limit. The winner is the person who produces the largest number of alternative or different ideas:

LIST ALL POSSIBLE USES FOR A BALL OR BALLS (PING-PONG, TENNIS, BASKETBALL, BASEBALL, SOCCER, FOOTBALL, AND SO ON.

*And sometimes we look for one thing and
find another.*
—MIGUEL DE CERVANTES

#2: MORE THAN MEETS THE EYE

One of the most useful of all thinking modes and one that is invaluable in creative problem-solving is visual thinking. It is especially useful in solving problems in which shapes, forms, or patterns are concerned. Yet, it is often poorly developed.

To improve your your powers of visualization, concentrate on the following illustration and use your imagination.

The question usually asked in connection with this design is whether you see the two figures: the vase and the two profiles. Go beyond the traditional fixed perception and try to see and imagine at least 8 to 12 different things. Look at the picture from many different points of view and from as many angles as you wish.

WHAT ELSE CAN YOU SEE IN THIS PICTURE?

> *We can have facts without thinking, but we cannot have thinking without facts.*
> —JOHN DEWEY

#3: PAIRING UP

Creative people usually form good, clear, sharp impressions of things they observe around them. As a result, the accumulated information in their memory storage is substantial. And they can easily retrieve the needed information when called upon to do so. Readily recallable information is essential for creative functioning.

This game, which you can play either solo or with with others, helps you to increase your facility of recall.

LIST ALL THE THINGS YOU CAN THINK OF THAT CAN COME IN PAIRS.

Examples
Shoes, gloves, socks

#4: HOW OB(LI)VIOUS I

Although the creative person likes the challenge of the complex, chaotic, difficult, and disorderly, he doesn't overlook the obvious and simple. If a problem can be solved in a simple, elegant, or economical way, he is not inclined to overcomplicate matters to achieve a complex solution.

The modern tendency, however, is to frequently search for the complicated when a simple solution would be sufficient. We are so overconditioned to look for, and develop, complex processes that we have become almost blind to what is frequently "obvious."

The following set of twenty classic mini-problems has been designed to test and develop your capacity to extract the obvious solutions from situations that at first glance seem somewhat complicated. Although you should figure out the problem quickly, try to inhibit your tendency to form snap judgments of what is involved.

1. You go to bed at 8 o'clock in the evening and set the alarm to get up at 9 in the morning. How many hours of sleep would this allow you?
2. One month has 28 days. Of the remaining 11 months, how many have 30 days?
3. A woman gave a beggar 50 cents. The woman is the beggar's sister, but the beggar is not the woman's brother. What is their relationship?
4. Why can't a man living in New York, N.Y., be buried west of the Mississippi?
5. Do they have a fourth of July in England?
6. How can you throw a tennis ball with all your might and have it stop and come right back to you without hitting any wall, net, or any other obstruction?
7. If you stand on a hard marble floor, how can you drop a raw egg five feet without breaking its shell?

8. Two fathers and two sons shot three deer. Yet each took home one deer. How was that possible?
9. How many times can you subtract the numeral 2 from the numeral 24?
10. A farmer has 4⁷/₉ haystacks in one corner of the field and 5²/₉ haystacks in another corner of his field. If he puts them all together, how many haystacks will he have?
11. Seven gas-guzzling cars were lined up in a dealer's showroom bumper-to-bumper. How many bumpers were actually touching each other?
12. Would it be cheaper for you to take one girlfriend to the movies twice or two girlfriends at the same time?
13. Take 5 apples from 7 apples and what have you got?
14. Was the old coin-dealer who said he had a silver coin marked 459 B.C. either lying or trying to put one over on the customer? If "Yes," why?
15. You won a prize in a contest and could choose either a truckload of nickels or half a truckload of dimes. Which would you choose? (Both trucks are identical in size and shape.)
16. Visualize four horizontal lines, one inch apart, one above the other. Now visualize four vertical lines, one inch apart, each cutting through the horizontal lines. How many squares did you form? (Do not use paper or pencil.)
17. Six robbers rode in a Chevette for over 150 miles to their hideout. The trip took exactly two hours, yet no one in the car noticed that they had a flat tire all this time. How was this possible?
18. The attempt to commit a certain crime is punishable, but the successful execution of the crime is never punishable. What crime is involved?
19. You are sitting in a room with 12 friends. Can any of them seat themselves in any particular place in this room where it would be impossible for you to do so?
20. After a woman was blindfolded, a man hung up her hat. She walked 50 meters, turned around, and shot a bullet through her hat. How was she able to do this?

By logic and reason we die hourly; by
imagination we live.
—W. B. YEATS

#5: TANTALIZING TANS

This fascinating Chinese game, called Tangrams, expands and enriches your imagination. There are over 1,600 design possibilities that can be constructed with one 7-piece set.

Basically, there are three categories of Tangram play. One is to use your ingenuity and sense of humor to construct as many shapes and designs as possible. Another is to duplicate complex shapes shown only in outline. The third method of play is intended for mathematicians to puzzle out various geometric problems.

Tangram began in China around 1800, and then spread rapidly westward. No one seems to know precisely how the word originated. One colorful and probably apochryphal story is that the name was derived from the Cantonese riverboat *tanka* girls who, in order to divert the amatory attentions of foreign sailors, taught them how to play the game.

In addition to challenging your imagination, Tangram is ideally suited to exercise your patience, concentration, and perceptual intelligence in understanding and manipulating various shapes. It is a game that can be enjoyed alone or with friends and family.

MAKE A LARGE COPY OF THIS SQUARE AND CUT APART ON THE HEAVY LINES. CAN YOU ARRANGE THE PIECES (TANS) TO FORM THESE DANCERS? ALL SEVEN PIECES MUST BE USED IN CREATING EACH FIGURE.

UTILIZING ALL SEVEN PIECES, CREATE: (1) A HOUSE (2) A PLANT (3) A BIRD (4) AN ANIMAL (5) AN OBJECT (6) A WEAPON (7) YOUR INITIALS (8) NUMERALS FROM 0 TO 9 (9) A HUMAN FIGURE—SITTING (10) A HUMAN FIGURE—RUNNING (11) A HUMAN FIGURE—FALLING (12) THREE GEOMETRIC FIGURES

Genius is the capacity for seeing relationships
where lesser men see none.
—WILLIAM JAMES

#6: CLOSE ASSOCIATES

Creativity is that process which results in a new combination or association of attributes, elements, or images, giving rise to new patterns, arrangements, or products that better solve a need. This is a condensation of several hundred definitions of the process of creative thinking, and the noteworthy element of almost all the definitions is that they emphasize the associative or combinational aspect of the creative process.

Creative men and women have described their creative thought-processes in associative terms. Albert Einstein said, "The psychical entities which seem to serve as elements of thought are certain signs and more or less clear images which can be combined. . . . This combinatory play seems to be the essential feature in productive thought." Samuel Taylor Coleridge, reflecting upon his own creative process, stated, "Facts which sank at intervals out of conscious recollection drew together beneath the surface through the almost chemical affinities of common elements." Similarly, André Breton remarked: "Creativity is a marvelous capacity to grasp two mutually distinct realities, without going beyond the field of our experience, and to draw a spark from their juxtaposition."

Most lucid and explicit is the statement by the mathematician Jules Poincaré, who said, "To create consists of making new combinations of associative elements which are useful. The mathematical facts worthy of being studied . . . are those which reveal to us unsuspected kinships between other facts well known but wrongly believed to be strangers to one another." And Jacob Bronowski added, "The discoveries of science, the works of art, are explorations—more, are explosions—of a hidden likeness."

This exercise is designed to stimulate this all-important ability to form associative elements. Take all the time you need to complete it.

Part I
THINK OF A WORD THAT PRECEDES THOSE IN THE

FIRST TWO COLUMNS AND FOLLOWS THOSE IN THE LAST TWO. (YOU CAN FORM COMPOUNDS, HYPHENATED WORDS, COMMONLY USED EXPRESSIONS, COLLOQUIAL USAGE, OR SLANG IN SOME CASES.)

Examples

BREAK	STRINGS	Heart	PURPLE	TAKE
SELL	ROCK	Hard	WORK	HIT

1. RATE	ACCOUNT	_____	SAVINGS	LEFT
2. SALAD	HEAD	_____	LAY	ROTTEN
3. CORNER	ROPE	_____	SIT	HOLD
4. OPERA	HOUSE	_____	FLASH	FLOOD
5. ARTIST	CLAUSE	_____	NARROW	FIRE
6. JACKET	CHANG-ER	_____	WORLD	OFF
7. DOG	SKIN	_____	HERDS	COUNT
8. IN	UGLY	_____	SPARK	DRAIN
9. OX	BUNNY	_____	DEAF	STRIKE
10. BACKER	DRAW-ING	_____	FISHING	TELE-PHONE
11. SHOOTING	DOOR	_____	SHUT	TOURIST
12. WARE	FOOT	_____	FALL	A
13. STEP	FLESH	_____	WILD	COOK
14. UP	GUY	_____	PENNY	SIDE
15. PARK	LIFE	_____	DAILY	PLAY
16. PIE	CART	_____	ROTTEN	CRAB
17. FALL	CAP	_____	GOOD	CHRIST-MAS
18. AIR	TUB	_____	GET	BOILING
19. OFF	TOE	_____	HOT	FINGER
20. BOOK	POINT	_____	RAIN	DOUBLE
21. RAGE	LOOK	_____	WASH	REACH
22. DAY	THEORY	_____	MAGNETIC	PLAYING
23. FINGER	LEADER	_____	BATHTUB	KEY
24. PAY	THROW	_____	ALL	STAY
25. OUT	PAN	_____	CZAR	SAINT

Part II
THINK OF A WORD THAT MAY BE INSERTED IN THE BLANKS BELOW TO FORM NEW WORDS.

Example

_____ba, _____mage, _____my, _____or, _____pus, _____runner

Answer: RUM

1. _____al, _____rabbit, _____et, _____frost, _____knife, _____pot

2. _____acid, _____arctic, _____elope, _____ler, _____hology, _____hem

3. _____an, _____bug, _____id, _____bled, _____or, _____us

4. _____cat, _____al, _____uity, _____head, _____igue, _____ten

5. _____alyst, _____atonia, _____ch, _____ty, _____nip, _____skill

6. _____ad, _____ast, _____istics, _____oon, _____ot, _____point

7. _____ace, _____ate, _____ette, _____lor, _____sy, _____try

8. _____er, _____beat, _____ice, _____end, _____hand, _____key

> *Men and women one of these days will have the courage to be eccentric. They will do as they like—just as the great ones have always done. The word eccentric is a term of reproach and mild contempt and amusement today, because we live under a system which hates real originality.*
> —HOLBROOK JACKSON

#7: DOODLES GAME

Here is your chance to exercise the more esoteric and zanier aspects of your imagination. It will also improve your ability to deduce the whole of an object or picture from its component parts.

This is a fun game to play with friends. Everyone present will be surprised at some of the witty, impertinent, intriguing, and clever interpretations that are apt to occur. Remember to change your perspective as you try to decipher the doodles—this will enable you to associate aspects of your imagination and experience in many unique ways.

GUESS WHAT THE FOLLOWING DOODLES REPRESENT.

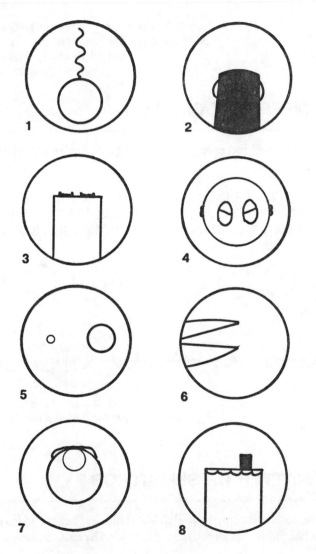

1. Top view of flag and flagpole
   A stubborn yo-yo
   A baby's head with a long curl of hair

*Effective learning means arriving at new
power, and the consciousness of new power is
one of the most stimulating things in life.*
—JANET ERSKINE STUART

#8: DIFFERENT CIRCLES

This exercise will increase your visual-figural acuity and your verbal fluency.

ADD *VERTICAL* LINES TO THE CIRCLES AND CREATE AS MANY WORDS AS YOU CAN. COPY AS MANY CIRCLES ON A PIECE OF PAPER AS YOU NEED TO FORM THE WORDS.

Examples

*The dictionary is a great book; it hasn't
much plot, but the author's vocabulary is
wonderful!*
—BILL NYE

#9: MATTER OF SEMANTICS

Creative people not only have rich vocabularies, but they also know how to handle words effectively. This effectiveness is due to their knowledge of the precise meaning of words, which contributes to conceptual clarity.

Clear and firm concepts are the building blocks to further creative learning and problem solving.

FROM THE FOUR POSSIBILITIES, SELECT THE ONE THAT MOST CLOSELY APPROXIMATES THE MEANING FOR EACH WORD AT THE LEFT.

1. felicitous — neat elegant congruous appropriate
2. jovial — blithe hearty merry sunny
3. tenacity — cohesion firmness persistence strength
4. alacrity — energy briskness activity readiness
5. simulate — mimic reflect counterfeit feign
6. recondite — tortuous occult furtive abstruse
7. frustrate — hinder thwart spoil outwit
8. emanate — appear exude issue proceed
9. bombastic — turgid explosive high-flown swollen
10. palliate — soften mitigate smooth relieve
11. theory — postulate hypothesis conjecture principle
12. stricture — compression narrowing obloquy criticism
13. expound — preach instruct edify interpret
14. equivocal — perplexing ambiguous mysterious obscure
15. mien — attitude bearing conduct action
16. fidelity — equality probity uniformity loyalty
17. sagacious — shrewd penetrating sensible rational
18. refractory — tenacious stubborn firm sullen
19. obdurate — unfeeling stubborn firm stern
20. tentative — fortuitous empirical experimental makeshift
21. esoteric — unusual bookish profound erudite
22. relegate — banish consign transpose promote
23. ephemeral — elusive fugitive passing transitory
24. cynical — arrogant sneering sarcastic haughty
25. sentient — quick keen sensitive emotional
26. explicit — definite positive manifest open
27. amorphous — formless misshapen unshapely malformed
28. dissident — dissonant improper discordant differing
29. perspicacity — shrewdness intelligence wisdom discernment
30. fortitude — bravery courage firmness valor

10: CELEBRATION

Experiments have indicated that creative individuals perform better on tests where words, shapes, and figures have somehow been camouflaged. See if you can penetrate the following camouflage.

THESE FIVE PIECES OF STEEL SCULPTURE, MOUNTED ON A MARBLE BASE, WERE CREATED BY A SCULPTOR BECAUSE HE WANTED TO CELEBRATE SOMETHING. WHAT MESSAGE DID HE HIDE IN THESE PIECES?

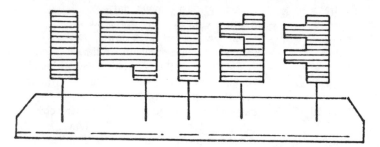

It is in games that many men discover their paradise.
—ROBERT LYND

11: CREATE A GAME

This exercise asks you to take on the role of a game designer. It challenges your inventiveness to camouflage or hide words inside other words. Your ingenuity will be twisted by the difficulty your friends will experience as they try to identify the hidden words in the sentences you construct. Game construction is not only fun; many consider it to be a highly creative art form.

CREATE SENTENCES WHICH WOULD CONCEAL THE FOLLOWING GAMES, SPORTS, OR DANCES.

Examples
Discus. I find these *discus*sions very boring. *Rowing.* After she had shot the ar*row, Ing*rid put her dark glasses in her pocket. *Lotto.* You must like her a *lot to* put up with so much.

If you want to be really creative, try hiding three or more games in one sentence.

Example
There is a *lot to* bother anyone about Jane, but he*r owing* so much money to Jack is really the reason why Mau*d is cus*sing and fuming so much.

NOW IT'S YOUR TURN TO HIDE THESE:

1. Polo	7. Wrestling	13. Badminton
2. Dice	8. Shotput	14. Lacrosse
3. Samba	9. Rugby	15. Golf
4. Track	10. Canasta	16. Scrabble
5. Bingo	11. Tennis	17. Archery
6. Poker	12. Boxing	18. Domino

(You may add additonal games or sports of your own choosing.)

> *Creativity is looking at a problem or a situation in a different way from everybody else and seeing something that they have missed. The trait can be cultivated by refusing to accept the obvious.*
> —Yurjio Yanamoto

#12: LOOSE STRINGS

Problems are situations that most people find uncomfortable, if not unpalatable. When confronted with a dilemma, the natural inclination is to seek, as quickly as possible, the simplest solution, and then move on to something else. People often jump to conclusions even before they have a full understanding of the situation. A poorly analyzed problem, however, invariably results in an inadequate or wrong response.

When a problem fails to yield a quick answer, many people doggedly stick to the one avenue of approach they have chosen and are unable to let go of it. A good problem-solver, on the other hand, turns the problem over on all sides, restates it several times, inhibits the tendency to persist in one direction, and deliberately experiments with a multitude of approaches. By deferring early commitment to one approach, he keeps his mind and his options open.

This exercise is an excellent means to become aware, and then overcome, this serious barrier to problem solving. Remember to restate the problem in many ways, and try to get the total picture in terms of feasible solutions before you actually tackle it.

LOOK AT THE SKETCH BELOW AND IMAGINE THAT YOU ARE THE PERSON SHOWN STANDING IN THIS ROOM. YOU HAVE BEEN GIVEN THE TASK OF TYING TOGETHER THE ENDS OF THE TWO STRINGS SUSPENDED FROM THE CEILING. THE STRINGS ARE LOCATED SO THAT YOU CANNOT REACH ONE STRING WITH YOUR OUTSTRETCHED HAND WHILE HOLDING THE SECOND IN YOUR HAND. UNLIKE PROBLEM #5, "LOOSE ENDS," IN *CREATIVE GROWTH GAMES*, IN WHICH THE ROOM WAS TOTALLY BARE, YOU CAN NOW IMAGINE THAT THE ROOM CONTAINS ALL THE THINGS YOU MIGHT NEED FOR SOLVING THE PROBLEM. TRY TO FIND AS MANY DIFFERENT SOLUTIONS AS YOU CAN. THERE IS NO TIME LIMIT.

*The thinking you do before you start a job
will shorten the time you have to spend
working on it.*
—ROY L. SMITH

#13: JOINED TOGETHER

To solve a problem creatively, we frequently need to step back to properly analyze and organize it, to determine the best method of approach. Most people rush to tackle a problem without considering the alternatives and without really attempting to understand what is involved. As the result, they waste a lot of time and effort.

COPY THIS DESIGN AND KEEP TRACK OF HOW LONG IT TAKES YOU. TRACING IS NOT ALLOWED.

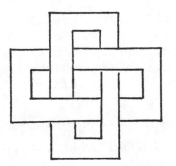

If it took you a minute, or over a minute, try a different approach, another point of view, and copy it again to see if that new point of view helps you copy it more quickly.

#14: APHORISTIC DEFINITIONS

Dictionary definitions lean more toward the conceptual and abstract. They often convey only desiccated meanings from which all but a pinpointing precision has been eliminated. Consequently they often seem rather inconsequential and leave a feeling of incompleteness in the mind of the reader.

Good aphoristic definitions, on the other hand, pack a force that ineluctably turn the reader to the experiential, to the immediately felt unique quality and flavor of life: experiences and happenings. By giving us a different and vivid slice of reality, they appeal to our imagination, interests, and values. They also come closer to capturing and conveying the real meaning of a word or situation, and are more provocative of thoughts than dictionary definitions.

This exercise is expressly designed to train your ability to add your own idiosyncratic quality and flavor to your observations of life experiences. It is an excellent and stimulating game to play with others, but choose partners who are not afraid to express their individuality.

PICK FIVE WORDS FROM THE FOLLOWING LIST AND WRITE YOUR OWN ORIGINAL, CONCISE DEFINITIONS FOR EACH WORD.

1. Advertising	10. Executive	19. A pessimist
2. Argument	11. Failure	20. A politician
3. Block	12. A friend	21. Procrastination
4. A bore	13. Gratitude	22. Progress
5. Conceit	14. Happiness	23. Reality
6. A cynic	15. Initiative	24. Self-evident
7. Depression	16. Life	25. Self-respect
8. Doctor	17. Luxury	26. Storyteller
9. Envy	18. Marriage	

#15: SIGHTWORDS

We usually express our thoughts in words. We can do it through
pictures, too.

This exercise helps you to develop your visual imagination—
your ability to express your thoughts in graphic ways.

FROM THE GIVEN LIST PICK THREE WORDS (OR AS
MANY AS YOU LIKE) YOU CAN WRITE IN A WAY THAT
EMPHASIZES THEIR MEANING. YOU MAY ALSO
CHOOSE YOUR OWN WORDS FOR THIS EXERCISE.

Hole	Mustache	Fraction	Delicate
Under	Sailor	Squeeze	Slope
Success	Gap	Circus	Foggy
Pastor	See	Balloon	Notes
Fish	Tie	People	Nose
Camel	Mountain	Blowout	Strong

Examples
Umbrella

*Creativity is a marvellous capacity to grasp
two mutually distinct realities without going
beyond the field of our experience and to
draw a spark from their juxtaposition.*
—Max Ernst

#16: AROUND THE CIRCLE

Creative problem-solving is frequently enhanced by the ability to take diverse objects, attributes, or phenomena and find a connecting principle or link that produces another object, attribute, or situation. This exercise is designed to increase your ability to make connections between various attributes.

THROW ONE DIE TO IDENTIFY THE FIRST ATTRIBUTE ON THE DIAL, THEN TWO TO GET THE SECOND. NOW CONNECT THE TWO ATTRIBUTES AND THINK OF THINGS THAT HAVE THEM BOTH.

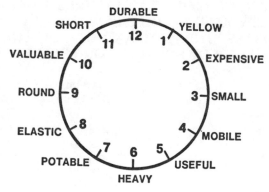

Example
Mobile (4) Round (9)

Wheel, gear, ball bearing, ball, earth, tire, circus, snowball, coin, pan, dishes, crystal ball, roll of toilet tissue

Habit and routine have an unbelievable power
to waste and destroy.
—HENRI DE LUBAC

#17: SQUARES APLENTY

Creativity frequently involves looking at a situation or a problem with fresh eyes and seeing in it something others have missed. This entails the refusal to accept the apparently obvious.

HOW MANY SQUARES DO YOU SEE?

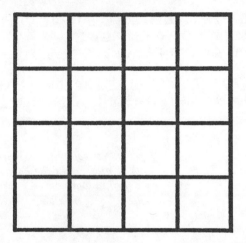

The "germ," wherever gathered, has ever been
for me "the germ of a story," and most of the
stories strained to shape under my hand have
sprung from a single small seed, a seed as
remote and windblown as a casual hint.
—HENRY JAMES

#18: TELL ME A STORY

For most people even the idea of telling a story turns their hands cold and sweaty and starts their stomachs flip-flopping. Yet, story-telling is one of the most effective ways of liberating and strengthening imagination.

If you feel inhibited about telling the story aloud, write it down. When playing this game with others, score a very good and original story (one that is either interesting, moving, amusing, or clever) 5 points, and a poor one 1 point.

VIVIDLY IMAGINE THE GIVEN OBJECTS IN FRONT OF YOU. THEN TELL (OR WRITE) A STORY ABOUT WHAT YOU SEE IN YOUR MIND'S EYE, USING AS GUIDES THESE THREE QUESTIONS:

1. WHAT PRECEDED OR LED UP TO THIS?
2. WHAT IS GOING ON NOW?
3. WHAT COULD THE OUTCOME BE?

BE SURE TO USE *ALL* THESE THREE QUESTIONS.
OBJECTS: AN OLD TROMBONE. A BROKEN DOLL.

> *Great minds comprehend more in a word, a look, a pressure of the hand than ordinary men in long conversations, or the most elaborate correspondence.*
> —Johann Lavater

#19: THE CONSCIENTIOUS DRIVER

Creative people possess the attribute of *cluency*, or the facility to make correct hypotheses and felicitous guesses that are based on only a few clues or hints. See if you can take a few short cuts and make an intuitive leap to the correct solution in this problem situation.

AUNT NELLIE ALWAYS FOLLOWED THE ADVICE TO CONSERVE ENERGY. WHILE DRIVING IN HER FAMILY FORD ONE DAY, SHE CAME TO A STOP SIGN AND NOTICED THAT THE ODOMETER SHOWED 25,952

MILES. OBSERVANT AS SHE WAS, SHE RECOGNIZED THAT THIS NUMBER WAS PALINDROMIC; IT READ THE SAME BACKWARD AS FORWARD.

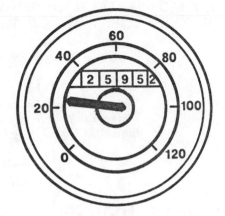

"I BET YOU IT'LL BE A LONG TIME BEFORE A PALIN-DROMIC NUMBER HAPPENS AGAIN," AUNT NELLIE SAID TO HERSELF. YET, TWO HOURS LATER WHEN SHE ARRIVED HOME THE ODOMETER SHOWED A NEW PALINDROMIC NUMBER.

WHAT WAS THE NEW PALINDROMIC NUMBER, AND HOW FAST WAS SHE TRAVELING IN THOSE TWO HOURS?

We put a rubber stamp on things and there it stays, often never to be removed.
—KURT HANKS

#20: CRAZY BUT NOT STUPID

Creative problem-solving often requires the ability to transcend conventional rules and regulations when it becomes appropriate or necessary.

See if you can solve this problem.

A MAN HAD A FLAT TIRE IN FRONT OF A NEUROPSY-CHIATRIC HOSPITAL. WHILE CHANGING TIRES HE LOST FOUR OF THE FIVE LUGS DOWN A NEARBY SEWER. HE WAS AT A LOSS AS TO WHAT TO DO UNTIL A PATIENT WHO HAD BEEN WATCHING SPOKE UP.

WHAT DID THE PATIENT ADVISE THE MAN TO DO?

> *The strictly logical mind is usually if not always at fault in its valuations of that defiantly illogical thing known as human nature.*
> —OSCAR W. FIRKINS

#21: TUESDAY'S TRANSACTIONS

One outstanding characteristic of effective problem-solvers is their ability to think of many different reasons, or justifications, for the happenings they observe around them. Only after they have considered all possibilities do they narrow them down to a few most likely or best explanations.

Poor problem-solvers, on the other hand, tend to be impatient and lazy. They cling to their first most apparent explanation and do not bother to go beyond it. Their perception of the world around them is, thus, often distorted and faulty. To solve a problem—almost any problem—successfully, you have to take the time to consider all the possible ramifications.

This exercise, of course, makes another good rainy-day party game.

Here is a statement which you are to *assume* is true and valid. Give as many plausible explanations as you can to explain the "truth" of this statement:

MORE IMPORTANT BUSINESS TRANSACTIONS ARE CONDUCTED ON TUESDAYS THAN ON ANY OTHER DAY OF THE WEEK.

*Our greatest weakness lies in giving up. The
most certain way to succeed is always to try
just one more time.*
—THOMAS EDISON

#22: THE MAGIC BOX

Changing circumstances frequently dictate that we reinterpret a
problem we're facing. See if you can make the alternative changes
and rearrangements required by this problem situation.

JACK RECEIVED FROM HIS RICH UNCLE IN BRAZIL A
BEAUTIFUL BOX LADEN WITH 36 AQUAMARINES,
TOURMALINES, AMETHYSTS, AND TOPAZES. JACK
LIKED THE BOX BECAUSE THE STONES WERE SO AR-
RANGED THAT EACH SIDE HAD EXACTLY 10 OF
THEM.

ONE DAY JACK'S OLDER BROTHER STOLE 4 OF THE
GEMS TO SUPPORT HIS DRUG HABIT. WHEN JACK DIS-
COVERED THAT THE GEMS WERE MISSING, HE SAID
TO HIS BROTHER, "DON'T WORRY, I CAN REGLUE THE
REMAINING 32 STONES SO THAT THERE WILL AGAIN
BE 10 OF THEM ON EACH SIDE.

NEXT WEEK 6 MORE STONES WERE MISSING, WITH
26 LEFT; THE WEEK AFTER, AN ADDITIONAL 2 STONES
HAD DISAPPEARED, WITH 24 REMAINING; AND THE
THIRD WEEK ANOTHER 2 WERE MISSING, WITH ONLY
22 STONES LEFT. BUT EACH TIME JACK FOUND A WAY

OF REDISTRIBUTING THE STONES SO THAT THERE WERE 10 ON EACH SIDE AS BEFORE.

CAN YOU FIND THE FOUR ARRANGEMENTS WITH 32, 26, 24, AND 22 STONES THAT JACK CAME UP WITH?

Nature gave men two ends—one to sit on and one to think with. Ever since then man's success or failure has been dependent on the one he used most.
—GEORGE R. KIRKPATRICK

#23: IDEA

This exercise goes beyond the training of expressional fluency and cognitive flexibility. According to the renowned psychologist J. P. Guilford, it enhances, albeit in somewhat rudimentary form, a person's organizing ability for such complex thinking as plots for novels, scientific theories, plans for new business organizations, or the building of any other systems which are comprised of many elaborately interrelated and interconnected parts.

This is another good game to play with friends. See how many sentences each of you can produce within a specified time limit, for example, 5 minutes.

WRITE FOUR-WORD SENTENCES FROM FOUR GIVEN LETTERS FOR EACH WORD:

I	D	E	A

Examples

| Immense | dogs | eat | avidly |
| I | don't | enjoy | apples |

NOW IT'S YOUR TURN. SEE HOW MANY SENTENCES YOU CAN PRODUCE.

#24: ADD MORE TO GET LESS

We frequently fail to solve problems because we have a tendency to jump into assumptions and form pre-judgments before we have had time to analyze what is involved. These unwarranted assumptions block our thinking processes and hamper our imaginations.

When doing this problem, try to defer any pre-judgments that may pop into your mind and try to deliberately change your point of view.

ADD ONE LINE TO THE ROMAN NUMERAL XXI (TWENTY-ONE) AND END UP WITH TWENTY. HOW MANY DIFFERENT SOLUTIONS CAN YOU COME UP WITH?

So long as there's a bit of a laugh going,
things are all right. As soon as this infernal
seriousness, like a greasy sea, heaves up,
everything is lost.
—D. H. Lawrence

#25: 'PUN MY WORD

Considerable empirical evidence suggests that people who are by nature playful and have a sense of humor are likely to be more imaginative and creative than those without these characteristics. Several tests utilizing wit, clever plays on words, and puns have been created to assess creative ability. The following game will challenge your punning ability. For extra fun and hilarity, play this game with a friend.

CREATE PUN-PHRASES THAT VARIOUS OCCUPATION-AL GROUPS COULD USE ON THEIR BUSINESS CARDS.

Examples
> TAILOR—My business is sew, sew.
> BAKER—I'm in the dough.
> STRIPTEASERS—We grind it out, or, We have nothing to hide.

In a similar fashion, create phrases for: florist, upholsterer, farmer, electrician, carpenter, shoemaker, garbage collector, fireman, preacher, IRS clerk, dairy farmer, toiletseat manufacturer, astronomer, basketball player, surgeon, mortician, miller, dynamite salesman, deep-sea diver, banker, pharmacist, plus any other occupation you can think of.

> *We would accomplish many more things if*
> *we did not think of them as impossible.*
> —CHRÉTIEN MALESHERBES

#26: COIN SHIFT

This classic parlor puzzle illustrates the rigidity with which most people approach problem situations. Traditionally, only one solution was thought to be possible for this problem. Nevertheless you can come up with several ingenious ones if you use your imagination.

SET A DIME BETWEEN TWO QUARTERS WITH ITS EDGES TOUCHING BOTH. NOW GET THE RIGHT-HAND QUARTER INTO THE MIDDLE POSITION WITHOUT MOVING THE DIME OR TOUCHING THE LEFT-HAND QUARTER.

*The common idea that success spoils people
by making them vain, egoistic and self-
complacent is erroneous; on the contrary, it
makes them, for the most part, humble,
tolerant, and kind. Failure makes people
bitter and cruel.*
—W. Somerset Maugham

#27: SUCCESS AND FAILURE

This game is designed to enhance your associational and expressional fluency. Played with friends, it becomes not just useful, but exciting and instructive as well. You are apt to have insight-expanding discussions of the varied meanings which people have for success and failure.

THINK UP FOURTEEN WORDS FOR WHICH THE SEVEN-LETTER WORDS *SUCCESS* AND *FAILURE* WOULD BE THE ACRONYMS. ALL WORDS SHOULD REFLECT IN SOME WAY YOUR CONCEPTION OF WHAT SUCCESS AND FAILURE MEAN TO YOU.

Examples
   To me these spell

SUCCESS		*FAILURE*	
Steadfastness	Energy	Fickleness	Unawareness
Understanding	Self-determination	Anger	Recklessness
Courage	Soundness	Irresponsibility	Egotism
Courteousness		Laziness	

Either I will find a way, or I will make one.
—Sir Philip Sidney

#28: DON'T FENCE ME IN

In *Creative Growth Games* you were posed with the challenge of connecting nine dots with four straight lines. If you have a good memory and remember the principle that led to the solution, you should not experience inordinate difficulty in solving these puzzles.

Good memory storage contributes significantly to almost all creative operations. It was valued so highly by the ancient Greeks that they created a special goddess named Mnemosyne to honor it.

If you missed the golden opportunity of reading *Creative Growth Games*, you might find solving these puzzles not especially easy. They illustrate how we sometimes impose too many subconscious constraints upon our problems and thus remain within their obvious boundaries (in the case of the puzzles, within the imaginary square and rectangular-shaped boundaries formed by the dots). Effective solutions to most of our problems require that we look at them in a broader perspective and have the courage to "kick the fences."

1. DRAW *SIX* STRAIGHT LINES (WITHOUT LIFTING THE PEN FROM THE PAPER AND WITHOUT RE-TRACING) THAT WILL CROSS THROUGH ALL SIXTEEN DOTS.

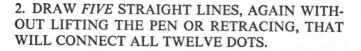

2. DRAW *FIVE* STRAIGHT LINES, AGAIN WITHOUT LIFTING THE PEN OR RETRACING, THAT WILL CONNECT ALL TWELVE DOTS.

· • • •

· • • •

· • • •

It better befits a man to laugh at life than to lament over it.
—Seneca

#29: HUMOROUS TITLES

Creativity involves the ability to penetrate the essence of a problem and discern through the clutter and teeming complex of superficial elements the crux of a situation.

In a similar fashion, when dealing with people the creative individual is able to focus on the more fundamental characteristics of a person and cast the superfluous aside. We see this, for example, in the works of good political cartoonists. Not only are they able to highlight the unique physical attributes of their subjects, but they somehow capture the essence of their personalities as well.

Because cartooning involves a special artistic talent, this game was designed to provide an equivalent exercise in verbal terms. Adding humor will enable you to cast the selected characteristics in bold relief.

THINK UP HUMOROUS TITLES FOR BOOKS OR ARTICLES CERTAIN CELEBRITIES COULD WRITE. (YOU MAY CHOOSE YOUR OWN "CELEBRITIES" OR TRY YOUR HAND WITH RICHARD NIXON, HENRY KISSINGER, JIMMY CARTER, DOLLY PARTON, OR OTHERS)

Examples

Nixon: "Reporters, Publishers, and Other Fiends"
  Nixon & Parton (co-authors): "The Perils of Full Disclosure"
Carter: "From Peanuts to President and Back"
  Kissinger: "The Source of Man's Wisdom: My Voice"

> *The greatest undeveloped asset in the world*
> *today is man's thinking. Surely it is up to us*
> *to at least get our own thinking on the right*
> *basis. No one else can do it for us.*
> —William Ross

#30: WORD CHANGE

This game exercises your powers of association and memory.

Here are two sets of words that have nothing in common except perhaps the implied thought that you take CARE of your MIND when you exercise it, and that to WRITE effectively you'll have to THINK.

BEGINNING WITH THE WORD CARE, CHANGE JUST *ONE* LETTER TO FORM A NEW WORD ON LINE 2. THEN CONTINUE CHANGING ONLY ONE LETTER AT A TIME TO ARRIVE AT THE WORD MIND ON LINE 5. FOLLOW THE SAME PROCEDURE WITH THE WORDS WRITE AND THINK.

1. CARE
2.
3.
4.
5. MIND

1. WRITE
2.
3.
4.
5. THINK

> *Most new discoveries are suddenly-seei*
> *things that were always there. A new idea is*
> *a light that illuminates presences which*
> *simply had no form for us before the light*
> *fell on them.*
> —SUSAN K. LANGER

#31: LIKE/UNLIKE

The ability to see similarities and differences between entities and objects is very important in creative problem-solving. Objects can be grouped together on the basis of some common features or attributes. Classification helps us to organize information, and it plays a significant role in memory and other thought processes. But equally important is the ability to make fine-tuned distinctions between things that look similar or belong to a certain class.

This exercise gives you an opportunity to train your ability to examine situations from different viewpoints and to process information flexibly in various ways.

Part I
HOW MANY COMMON FEATURES OR PROPERTIES CAN YOU FIND IN THE TWELVE GIVEN LETTERS?

There are at least twelve possible classifications of at least four letters each.

ZXTSNKHEDCBJ

Example

SDCBJ   Contain curved lines

TNKHEDB   Contain vertical straight lines

NOW FIND THE TEN REMAINING GROUPINGS.

Part II
GIVE AN EXPLANATION WHY *EACH* OF THE TWELVE LETTERS DOES NOT BELONG WITH THE OTHER ELEVEN.

Example
Z is the only one with two parallel horizontal lines.

NOW STATE HOW EACH OF THE LETTERS (INCLUDING ANOTHER EXPLANATION FOR z) IS DIFFERENT FROM THE REST OF THE GIVEN LETTERS.

> *There are few satisfactions in life that can compare with the knowledge that you have obtained some mastery over words.*
> —MELVIN H. MILLER

#32: IN OTHER WORDS

Only a few individuals fully utilize the potential of our wondrously versatile language. Most are content to take refuge in communication that is frequently stereotyped, trite, cliché-ridden, and repetitious.

Although there are literally thousands of options in word usage and idiom, rare indeed is the man or woman who has the requisite zest for the language to search for and capture the right words to convey the unique nuance of an image or situation.

Creative and original communication requires not only the knowledge of a rich array of words and synonyms, but the ability to distinguish and discriminate between them.

This exercise will increase your ability to be more creative and successful in your use of words.

LIST AS MANY WORDS AND PHRASES (INCLUDING SLANG AND COLLOQUIALISMS) AS YOU CAN THAT MEAN THE SAME, OR ALMOST THE SAME, AS THE WORD

FOOLISH

*Watch your step when you immediately know
the one way to do anything. Nine times out of
ten, there are several better ways.*
—WILLIAM B. GIVEN, JR.

#33: A PERFECT MATCH

Many problems needing creative solutions require that the elements
or parts of the problem be rearranged into a completely new pattern.

This exercise increases your fluency and flexibility to make
visual transformations.

IN THE FOLLOWING SERIES OF SEVEN PROBLEMS
YOU HAVE TO MOVE ONE OR MORE MATCHES TO A
DIFFERENT POSITION TO MAKE THE EQUATIONS COR-
RECT OR TO GET THE REQUIRED CONFIGURATIONS.

Example:
Matches are laid out in this pattern.

VII — II = II

Move two matches and make the equation valid.

Answers

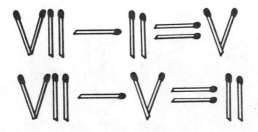

1. Move one match and make the equation valid. (There are at least two solutions.)

2. Move two matches to make a correct equation. (There are at least two solutions.)

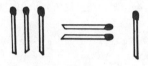

3. Three matches are on a table. Without adding another, make four out of them. You are not allowed to break the matches.

4. Make this roman numeral equation read correctly without touching a match.

5. From this row of six matches, shift two so as to leave nothing.

6. Here are three squares made of twelve matches.
   Take away one match and shift two to get one.

7. Make four squares with sixteen matches.

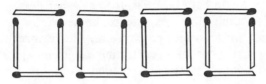

Now remove four matches and shift three to get "what perfect matches are made of."

You may not realize it when it happens, but a kick in the teeth may be the best thing in the world for you.
—WALT DISNEY

#34: WHAT'S GOOD ABOUT IT?

Most people, when they experience a serious disappointment or setback, or a situation which might "normally" and habitually be treated as a disaster, lapse into a very noncreative state of mind that sometimes lasts for several weeks or even months. The stages a person goes through when confronted with a grave problem consist of, first, denial or distortion of the true nature of the problem; second, anger-resentment directed toward those who allegedly caused the problem, and, finally, depression, which usually paralyzes thinking processes for a shorter or longer period.

Sidney X. Shore has come up with a seemingly simple but very effective method of short-circuiting the incapacitating period that follows a difficult situation. It consists of writing out all the things that are *good* about the difficult problem. This is not espousing a pollyanna attitude, for the efficacy and validity of this method has been proven in numerous creativity seminars.

These, typically, are the events that take place after a person starts responding to the question, "What's good about it?":

He or she sees the difficult (or impossible) situation in a new and different light.

The person actually begins to find and see many beneficial and useful things inherent in the problem situation.

He finds numerous unique ways of turning that difficult situation around, and detects new advantages and possibilities in what ordinarily would have been regarded as a hopeless quandary.

As the result of this experience, he develops a new, creatively beneficial attitude toward problems. He replaces frantic hand-wringing with a cool and penetrating insight into problems in general and derives greater satisfaction from the challenges they pose.

He or she will find it much easier to carry out this process next time and will be strengthening a new creative and imaginative technique which will help generate new advantages out of almost any problem situation faced. By changing viewpoints and being non-judgmental, he has a ready tool to overcome negative thoughts and worries, and shift creative thinking and creative action into high gear.

LIST ALL THE POSSIBLE THOUGHTS AND IDEAS TO THE HYPOTHETICAL QUESTION "WHAT'S GOOD ABOUT BEING FIRED FROM YOUR JOB TOMORROW?"

Remember to defer judgment or any negative thoughts that might occur. Change viewpoints—look at the situation through your own as well as other people's eyes. Ask, "*How* and *why* is it good for me?" . . . "*How* and *why* is it good for anyone else I can think of?" Try to find at least a dozen "good" idea answers.

I invent nothing; I rediscover.
—Auguste Rodin

#35: OVALATION

Here is another chance for you to test and exercise your ability to retrieve and recall visual impressions from your memory storage.

DRAW AS MANY OBJECTS AS YOU CAN FROM AN
OVAL. THE OVAL SHAPE MAY BE PART OF AN OB-
JECT.

TIME LIMIT: 10 minutes.

> *Man must never be judged according to the*
> *category to which he belongs. The category is*
> *the most barbarous and diabolical aberration*
> *ever begotten by the human mind.*
> —G. V. GEORGHIU

#36: BOATRIDE

Creating clever, witty titles for short stories provides a real workout
for the imagination. Not only does a good title bring to focus the
central point of the story, but it has to be compact and precise. In
addition, it should arouse curiosity and interest in what the story is
all about.

LIST AS MANY POSSIBLE TITLES TO THIS STORY AS
YOU CAN.

An old sailor sometimes took people for trips in his rickety row-
boat. One day a professor of rhetoric hired him to row across a wide
lake. As soon as they had departed, the professor asked the sailor
whether it was going to be a rough journey.

"I don't know nuttin' about that," said the sailor.

"Have you never attended school?"

"Nope," said the sailor.

"In that case, half your life has been lost."

The sailor said nothing.

Soon a terrible storm was tossing the boat like crazy and it was
filling with water. The sailor shouted to his ashen-faced passenger,
"Have you ever learned to swim?"

"No," said the professor.

"In that case, professor, *all* your life is lost, for we are rapidly
sinking."

> *All problems become smaller if you don't dodge them, but confront them. Touch a thistle timidly, and it pricks you; grasp it boldly, and its spines crumble.*
> —WILLIAM S. HALSEY

#37: NUMBERS GAMES

Although the ten exercises in the following set are presented in numerical terms, they require no special mathematical training or aptitude.

Numbers-operations provide an excellent means for inventive manipulation and combination, and they involve several functions necessary for effective problem-solving: perception of symbolic relations, implications, and systems. With numbers you arrive at solutions you can easily check; with ideas it is not always possible to achieve consensual agreement.

1. Place numbers from 1 to 16 in the small squares so that each vertical, horizontal, and one diagonal column equals 34. Use *all* the numbers from 1 to 16, and each only once. Five numbers have been placed to get you off to a good start.

		3	
		10	
9			
	14		1

2. When my mother was 41 years old, I was 9. Now she is twice as old as I am. How old am I?

3. Here are two columns of numbers. The numbers in both columns are the same, but they are inverted and in reverse order in the right column. Can you tell at a glance which column has the larger total?

123456789	1
12345678	21
1234567	321
123456	4321
12345	54321
1234	654321
123	7654321
12	87654321
1	987654321

4. How can you make four 9's equal 100?

5. Using the same figure six times, how can you make them add up to 100?

6 Can you make eight 8's equal 1000?

7. Add the following numbers to obtain 1111. (There are several solutions.)

4 5 1 6 7 9 8

8. Express 100 with five 1's.

Express 100 three ways with five 5's.

9. Name the next number in this sequence.

77, 49, 36, 18,—

10. Three kinds of pears are mixed in a bag. How many pears must you take out to be sure that you have at least 2 pears of one kind? At least 3 pears of one kind?

*There is more power in a hint to the
imagination than there is in the satiety of
completed forms.*
—RADHAKAMAL MUKERJEE

#38: THUMBPRINT DRAWINGS

Even the simplest observations can trigger the imagination of creative people. Psychologist Dr. Kate Franck asked subjects to complete the simple figures below. At left are typical responses of subjects chosen at random; at right are the responses of creative individuals. As is apparent, there is an unmistakable tendency toward complexity, elaboration, whimsy, and imaginativeness on the part of creative individuals.

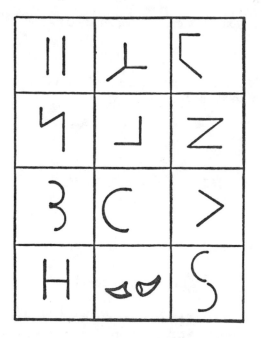

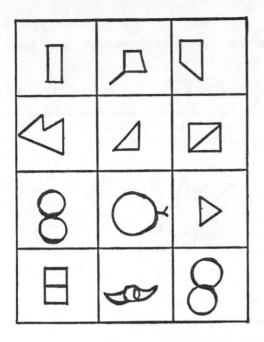

Here is your chance to be creative with even simple perceptual stimulus lines: your thumbprint.

MAKE A THUMBPRINT DRAWING; INK YOUR THUMB WITH A STAMP PAD, THEN PRESS YOUR THUMB ON A PIECE OF PAPER. WITH A FELT-TIPPED PEN, DRAW THE LINES THAT WILL CREATE A PICTURE.

Example

NOW INK TWO, THREE, OR ALL OF YOUR FINGERS, PRESS THEM ON PAPER AND DRAW ADDITIONAL PICTURES.

Be obscure clearly.
—E. B. WHITE

#39: SELECTIVE DIAGNOSTIC INDICATOR

The following are three columns of personality characteristics that you can use to diagnose the behavior or actions of friends or enemies with all the aplomb and erudition of a psychiatrist.

Think, for example, of your boss, or any other persons whom you consider "significant," and choose one word from each category to find the best combination of three words which describe that individual's behavior or personality.

1. Acute	1. Dysfunctional	1. Grandiosity
2. Borderline	2. Compensatory	2. Deficiency
3. Morbid	3. Compulsive	3. Rigidity
4. Presenile	4. Ambivalent	4. Fixation
5. Irrational	5. Punitive	5. Posture
6. Psychosexual	6. Depressive	6. Exhibitionism
7. Infantile	7. Narcissistic	7. Confusion
8. Antisocial	8. Paranoid	8. Illusion
9. Inhibited	9. Pathological	9. Complex
10. Moronic	10. Obsessive	10. Satyriasis
11. Distorted	11. Latent	11. Regression
12. Oral-Agressive	12. Maladaptive	12. Denial
13. Agitated	13. Masochistic	13. Verbigeration
14. Negativistic	14. Episodic	14. Delusion

Examples

Instead of saying that your boss, for example, goes off half-cocked all the time, you could pick numbers 1, 12, 13 from the respective columns and say that he's suffering from "acute maladaptive verbigeration."

About an uptight person you could use 14, 2, 3, and say that she exhibits "negativistic compensatory rigidity."

Obnoxious show-off behavior could become "infantile narcissistic grandiosity" (7, 7, 1).

A self-pitying middle-aged fogey could be diagnosed as having a "presenile masochistic posture" (4, 13, 5).

And someone who is too anxiously on the make could be said to show "agitated dysfunctional exhibitionism or satyriasis" (13, 1, 6, or 10).

> *Be not afraid of going slowly, be afraid only*
> *of standing still.*
> —CHINESE PROVERB

#40: PIE TIME

This problem tests your perseverance and stick-to-itiveness.

Eleven relatives of varying ages and appetites descend upon your house on a Sunday afternoon. You have only one large custard pie to divide among them.

How can you cut the pie in *eleven* parts—not necessarily of equal size—making just *four* straight-line cuts?

#41: PATTERNS OF THE MIND

One of the most useful instruments to measure originality and imagination is the inkblot test.

There are several response patterns that creative individuals exhibit:

They attempt the most difficult and far-reaching interpretation of the entire blot; one that incorporates the details in a comprehensive, synthesizing image. The less creative individuals, on the other hand, concentrate on small portions or details of the blots and fail to see the whole.

They have the ability to see unusual possibilities in the blots; ones that evoke complex associations in their minds. They thus give highly individualistic, original, and imaginative responses to the messy blots.

While interpreting the entire "scenes," they see some movement, some "happenings," in the figures, and typically relate a short story about what they're experiencing. The less creative give fewer movement responses and see things in a rigid, static way.

Although they have rich fantasies, the forms they perceive are clearly visualized and immediately apparent to others when pointed out. Less creative men and women frequently show poor form visualization, making it difficult for others to "see" the configurations they perceive.

Examples

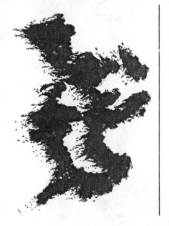  

Less Creative or Common Responses

Smudges	An ape	A cactus plant
Dark clouds	Modern painting of a gorilla	An African voodoo dancer
A woman	A grotesque person	A Chinese letter

More Creative or Uncommon Responses

Magnetized iron filings being pulled together by a magnet	An orchestra conductor scolding the cellist for playing a sour note	Mexican in sombrero running up a long hill to escape from rain clouds

A small boy and his mother hurrYing along on a dark, windy day, trying to get home before it rains

Rodin's "The Thinker" shouting, "Eureka!" as he finally solved his problem

Pluto in a ballet scene about to make the splits

A cook tossing a hot piece of meat as she tries to land it on a plate

A babboon admiring himself in a hand mirror

A woman trying to negotiate a puddle of water

As you interpret the two designs that follow, try to focus on the shapes as a whole. You may turn them sideways or upside down to change your viewpoint. Take your time and try for the most complete and imaginative responses you can produce.

The greatest thing by far is to be a master of metaphor.
—ARISTOTLE

#42: WHAT'S LOVE LIKE?

Simile and metaphor are two of the most ancient forms of speech. They have proven themselves essential to every form of human utterance. The Old Testament, for example, abounds in similes and metaphors that are now current coin: "Still as a stone," "White as snow," "Boil like a pot," "Unstable as water," "Sharp as a two-edged sword," "Melted like wax," and so on.

Similes and metaphors are not mere figures of speech, frills, or devices to vivify language. They are inextricably bound up with language and thought. They give us unique insights into reality and provoke new contexts for viewing the old and familiar.

COMPLETE THE FOLLOWING SIMILES INVOLVING LOVE.

Example: Love, like fire, . . .

Possible ending: . . . when once kindled, is soon blown into a
   flame.—HENRY FIELDING
Love is like a landscape . . . which doth stand,
   Smooth at a distance, rough at hand.—ARSÈNE HOUSSAYE
Love is like medical science . . . the art of assisting Nature.
   —LALLEMAND
Love, like flowers, . . . endureth but a spring.—RONSARD
Love is like a red-currant wine . . . it first tastes sweet,
   but afterward shuddery.—I. W. ROBERTSON

NOW TRY THESE

   Love is a fire . . .
   Love's like the measles—
   Love, like the creeping vine,
   Love, like cough,
   True love is like ghosts,
   Love is like the moon:
   Love is like a child,
   Love, like a pirate,
   Love, like fortune,
   Love, like ambition,
   Love is like linen,
   Love, like reputation,

*Undertake something that is difficult; it will
do you good. Unless you try to do something
beyond what you have already mastered, you
will never grow.*
—Ronald E. Osborn

#43: BOUNDARIES, SHAPES, AND SIZES

Here's another chance for you to tax your powers of visualization. The following visual-figural problems are designed to exercise a multitude of abilities important in creative problem-solving: spatial orientation, perceptual foresight of implications, adaptive flexibility, and figural restructuring and transformation. Although the tasks require operations that meet prescribed requirements, and have only one right answer, they demand considerable imaginative flexibility and ingenuity.

1. Trace the lines in this diagram without lifting the pen from the paper and without *retracing* any lines. You may begin at any spot of your choosing.

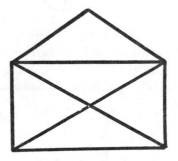

2. Arrange the seven dots so that they make five straight rows with three dots in each row.

3. Put these seven dots into seven squares. You're allowed to draw only three squares, and no more than four squares can be the same size.

4. A man had a very lucky horseshoe which he wanted to divide among his six sons. He did it by cutting only two straight lines. How did he do it?

5. Copy this design and cut it into three parts with two straight cuts, so that the individual parts when reassembled will form a square.

6. Copy this letter E, cut it into seven parts with four straight cuts, and form a square out of the parts.

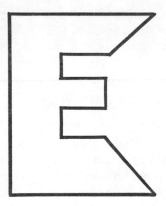

*To make ideas effective, we must be able to
fire them off.*
—Virginia Woolf

#44: NEWS HEADLINES

This exercise gives you another chance to increase your word fluency within certain constraints: each three-word "headline" must make use of alliteration, and it must sound like a headline.

Competing with friends will enable them also to loosen up their vocabularies and tone up creative imagination.

WRITE THREE-WORD "HEADLINES" THAT MIGHT APPEAR IN TOMORROW'S NEWSPAPER. BEGIN WITH THE LETTER A, THEN WITH THE REST OF THE VOWELS E, I, O, U. ALLOW FOUR MINUTES FOR EACH LETTER.

Examples
    A—Affluent Arabs Arrive
    E—Elephants Escape Extinction
    I—India's Independence Imperiled
    O—Official's Ouster Obstructed
    U—Unscrupulous Umpire Unmasked

NOW IT'S YOUR TURN.

*If I have ever made any valuable discoveries,
it has been owing more to patient attention,
than to any other talent.*
—Isaac Newton

#45: RADAR PALINDROME

The popular notion that the creative individual is one who relies mainly on effortless inspiration and easy spontaneity is still a widespread belief. It is not fully appreciated that creative work frequently requires painstaking attention, an obstinate persistence in the face of difficulties and frustrations, and a vast amount of arduous work. It takes a lot of unrelenting practice, patience, and perseverance to achieve ideational dexterity.

During armament negotiations in Europe, a general needed information on the exact number of early detection radar systems installed around the world. Since none of the secret codes could be trusted, he received this information in the form of the following palindrome. (A palindrome is a word that can be read from either end).

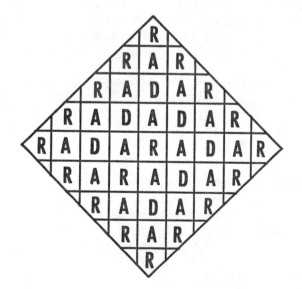

HOW MANY DIFFERENT WAYS CAN YOU LOCATE THE WORD *RADAR?*

You can place your pencil on any R, then move it to the adjoining A, and so on, until the word RADAR is spelled. Movements in all directions—up, down, sideways, or diagonally are allowed. You can return to letters previously used, such as reversing yourself from RAD back to the previously used AR. The only requirement is that you are not allowed to jump over, or omit, letters; you must continue to the next adjoining letter that is usable.

> *The test of a first-rate intelligence is the*
> *ability to hold two opposed ideas in the mind*
> *at the same time, and still retain the ability*
> *to function.*
> —F. Scott Fitzgerald

#46: POLARITIES

One distinguishing characteristic of creative people is that they often use many opposite associations, images, and concepts when formulating new approaches or solutions to problems. During the creative process their thinking readily oscillates between antithetical, or opposite, ideas, which are subsequently synthesized into a coherent, unified whole. This predisposition to think in opposites is almost an habitual and automatic response with creative people and is also evident in their performance on word-association tests: they consistently respond to stimulus words by giving their antonyms.

The following exercise is designed to train and facilitate your capacity in this mode of thinking.

GIVE THE OPPOSITES TO THE FOLLOWING WORDS, BEGINNING WITH THE LETTER A.

1. Timid	4. Scarce	7. Retard	10. Increase
2. Affinity	5. Relative	8. Opponent	11. Remote
3. Natural	6. Reject	9. Unfinished	12. Discard

13. Enlarge	17. Deny	21. Rational	24. Real
14. Consequent	18. Unreal	22. Certainty	25. Dissimilar
15. Fail	19. Deliberate	23. Cool	26. Gradual
16. Insufficient	20. Expend		

> *The obscure we see eventually, the completely*
> *apparent takes longer.*
> —EDWARD R. MURROW

#47: ODD ONE OUT

We must know the similarities and differences between objects and meanings, and ways to classify items of information before we engage in any meaningful problem-solving. Conceptual classification helps us organize information and identify correctly what we perceive.

Of course, there are numerous ways to classify objects and meanings, and creative people are especially adept at finding unique methods of approach. But this can be accomplished only after the primary classification is known. One has to know these basic categories before one can *break* them.

IN THE FOLLOWING LISTS OF FIVE WORDS, WHICH WORD DOES NOT BELONG TO THE SAME CLASS WITH THE REST?

1. Learning, erudition, achievement, scholarship, knowledge
2. Recognize, identify, know, admit, remember
3. Attract, enamor, bewitch, cherish, enchant
4. Constancy, resoluteness, stability, firmness, steadfastness
5. Vision, dream, phantasy, reverie, idea
6. Apology, excuse, penance, concession, regret
7. Intelligent, talented, sharp, bright, smart
8. Furious, exasperated, irate, enraged, incensed
9. Sorcery, charm, magic, astrology, spell
10. Devout, religious, reverent, pious, faithful
11. Internist, oculist, psychiatrist, gynecologist, urologist

12. Magazine, movies, radio, game, book
13. Index, classify, tabulate, list, systematize
14. Insight, perception, intuition, impression, apprehension

*Creativity involves breaking out of
established patterns in order to look at things
in a different way.*
—EDWARD DE BONO

#48: HOW OB(LI)VIOUS II

Many new ideas and inventions look so "obvious" after the fact that we frequently exclaim, "Why didn't I think of that?" A. L. Simberg, of General Motors, notes that the invention of a flexible ice cube tray was the result of an obvious situation. The individual responsible for it got the idea when he noticed that some water in his boots, which had been left outside, had frozen during the night and had flipped out easily when the boot was turned inside out. The history of inventions is replete with similar accidental and obvious discoveries.

This set of ten problems gives you yet another opportunity to liberate yourself from the habit of looking for a complex solution, when a simple one will suffice.

1. Larry is languishing in jail in Mexico. The jail has multiple locks on the door; the walls are made of concrete which extend two stories into the earth, and the floor is made of packed earth. In the middle of the ceiling, eight feet above Larry, is a skylight just wide enough for his emaciated body to squeeze through. The cell is totally bare, so there is nothing he can climb on to reach the skylight.

    One night, in desperation, he got an idea. He dug a hole in the floor and escaped through the skylight. How?

2. Erica was waiting for her boyfriend to pick her up in his brand new Jaguar. He was late; the sky clouded over and it suddenly started to rain. Erica had no umbrella, no hat, and she was far from any awning or canopy. Yet after a five-minute wait, when the boyfriend finally arrived, she

got into the car with her hair and clothes perfectly dry. How was that possible?

3. How could you put your left hand *completely* in your right-hand pants pocket, and your right hand *completely* in your left-hand pants pocket, both at the same time?

4. Two policemen stood behind a billboard to wait for speeding violators. One of them looked up the highway, the other looked down it, so as to cover all the six lanes. "Mike," said one without turning his head, "what the heck are you smiling at?" Explain how he could tell that Mike was smiling.

5. Sam bought a phonograph record which has a total diameter of 12 inches. The recording has an outer margin of half an inch; the diameter of the unused center of the record is 3 inches. There is an average of 100 grooves to the inch. How far does the stylus travel when the record is played?

6. Visualize three playing cards adjacent to one another. A four is just to the right of a three. Another four is just to the left of a four. There is a diamond just to the left of a heart, and a diamond just to the right of a diamond. Can you name the three cards?

7. There are, of course, 12 one-cent stamps in a dozen, but how many two-cent stamps are there in a dozen?

8. Jack bought an old horse and pig for $85. The horse cost $55 more than the pig. How much did Jack pay for the pig?

9. Name at least eight articles, each starting with the letter "s," worn on the feet.

10. There are 14 punctuation marks in English grammar. Can you name 10 of them?

Creativity is the production of meaning by synthesis.—DR. MYRON S. ALLEN

#49: WANT TO MAKE SOMETHING OF IT?

Creative individuals have the capacity to take a group of disparate elements or parts and combine them into an integrated whole. Once they are *orchestrated* into a complete figure, the separate elements become interdependent and interrelated so as to function in harmony.

TURN THE FOLLOWING TWO SETS OF LINES OR DRAWING FRAGMENTS INTO SOMETHING RECOGNIZABLE.

To complete these unfinished drawings, copy them on two sheets of paper. You may turn the sheets into any position you want. Use the lines so they become a coherent part of the total picture you produce. You don't have to have exceptional drawing ability to make the pictures; it's the idea in your mind's eye that counts.

This game is a good one to play with others. Drawings are evaluated and judged by all the participants. Give 5 points for a very original, intriguing, or unusual sketch, all the way down to 1 point for something that doesn't tie the fragments together very well or is lacking in imagination.

The ability to relate and to connect,
sometimes in odd and yet striking fashion,
lies at the very heart of any creative use of
the mind, no matter in what field or
discipline.
—GEORGE J. SEIDEL

#50: BUILD A BRIDGE

Creative imagination is enhanced when the association of ideas stimulates the formation of new concepts. This game increases your ability to identify, associate, and relate your ideas; it enlarges the scope of your associative powers.

FILL THE SPACES BETWEEN THE TWO WORDS IN
SUCH A WAY THAT EACH WORD IMPLIES, OR IS
MEANINGFULLY RELATED TO, THE WORD FOLLOW-
ING IT.

Example
1. Ice _____ out
   Possible Answer: Ice pick out
2. Folk _____ _____ _____ mattress
   Possible Answers: Folk music box spring mattress
3. Jet _____ _____ _____ _____ _____ avenue
   Possible Answers: Jet engine power play ball park avenue

Now it's your turn.
1. Old _____ shop
2. Fire _____ premium
3. Free _____ guy
4. Fish _____ book
5. Expense _____ number
6. Iron _____ _____ block
7. Sleep _____ _____ line
8. Minute _____ _____ maker
9. White _____ _____ _____ laundry
10. Brain _____ _____ _____ game
11. Power _____ _____ _____ brains
12. Black _____ _____ _____ remark
13. Shell _____ _____ _____ thing
14. Nuclear _____ _____ _____ _____ bag
15. Blank _____ _____ _____ _____ upon
16. Body _____ _____ _____ _____ jam
17 Nose _____ _____ _____ _____ time
18. Eagle _____ _____ _____ _____ _____ drums
19. Fuel _____ _____ _____ _____ _____ master
20. Land _____ _____ _____ _____ _____ power
21. Foul _____ _____ _____ _____ _____ _____ alarm
22. Hair _____ _____ _____ _____ _____ _____ scared

71

> *When change is rapid and problems abundant, society must be creatively adaptive, or fall further and further behind.*
> —David Moss

#51: EMPTY BOTTLE BINGE

The realization that we are a nation of untidy wasters is growing. We are not only wasteful of our natural resources, but also of our potential as creative human beings able to exercise our resourcefulness and imagination.

This exercise is designed to give you another chance to tax your imagination and augment your conceptual fluency and flexibility.

The polyethylene containers that household detergents and other chemicals come in are nearly all discarded. And they are virtually decay-proof (nonbiodegradable) products.

SUGGEST AS MANY USES AS POSSIBLE FOR EMPTY PLASTIC HOUSEHOLD DETERGENT BOTTLES.

Example
    Cut off top section and use as a funnel.

#52: DISCERNMENT

As the title implies, this exercise improves your powers of discernment and recognition.

It is also a good test of concentration and perseverance. Many individuals fail at creative undertakings not because they lack talent, but because they lack the qualities of patient attention and persistence. Build the habit of persistence and you get the habit of victory.

MAKE AS MANY DIFFERENT WORDS AS YOU CAN, USING ONLY THE LETTERS THAT APPEAR IN THE WORD

D I S C E R N M E N T

IN ANY WORD YOU MAKE, FROM 3 LETTERS TO 11 LETTERS, EACH LETTER IN *DISCERNMENT* MAY BE USED ONLY AS MANY TIMES AS IT APPEARS. YOU MAY NOT USE FOREIGN WORDS, ABBREVIATIONS, CONTRACTIONS, OR SLANG.

Example

For the word CREATIVITY:

Tea	Rite	React	Treaty
Eat	Tart	Rivet	Trivia
Era	Tear	Tacit	Verity
Are	Very	Trace	Vitiate
Rat	Vice	Trait	Variety
Arty	Year	Trice	Activate
Aver	Cater	Vicar	Veracity
Care	Crate	Attic	Activity
Cart	Evict	Active	Reactivity
Cave			

#53: HORSING AROUND

Viewpoint change is one of the most powerful techniques for solving problems and generating ideas. It is also one that most people are unaccustomed to, as is illustrated by the following problem that seems to stump those who try it.

COPY THE FOLLOWING THREE DESIGNS AND CUT THE COPIES OUT EXACTLY AT THE DOTTED LINES. NOW SEE IF YOU CAN ARRANGE THE THREE PIECES SO THAT YOU HAVE THE TWO JOCKEYS MOUNTED *UPRIGHT* ON THE TWO HORSES.

#54: EMPATHETIC SENSITIVITY

One of the most important attributes of the creative person is his or her ability to perceive and notice needs, events, and challenges that have escaped the attention of other individuals.

This exercise is designed to develop your ability to see problems and implications in the area of interpersonal relations.

WHAT PERSONAL PROBLEMS CAN A HUSBAND AND WIFE HAVE WITH EACH OTHER? IN EXACTLY FIVE MINUTES LIST AS MANY PROBLEMS AS YOU CAN.

Examples

Husband dislikes wife's friends.
Wife makes fun of husband's sloppy habits.
Husband is jealous of wife's popularity with men.
Wife craves much body contact and silent communication, but the husband likes to talk a lot.
Husband needs to be constantly praised, but the wife wishes to be praised also.

> *You must love your work as you love a mistress whom you want to glorify. Once you are possessed by the creative urge there is no room for any other drive or thought.*
> —CARL HAUPTMANN

#55: A LOVING CODE

Here is another chance for you to tax your ingenuity in penetrating a camouflaged message. The exercise illustrates how much creative juggling the brain has to do in perceiving things.

A YOUNG MATHEMATICS PROFESSOR WAS VERY SMITTEN WITH A GRADUATE STUDENT. BECAUSE OF HIS EXCESSIVE SHYNESS AND FEAR OF REJECTION, HE COULDN'T OPENLY DECLARE HIS FEELINGS. ONE DAY HE ASKED THE STUDENT TO STAY AFTER CLASS TO SOLVE A PROBLEM. WHEN THE STUDENT SAW THE MESSAGE ON THE BLACKBOARD, SHE IMMEDIATELY RECOGNIZED WHAT IT MEANT, FOR SHE SHARED HIS FEELINGS. CAN YOU TRANSLATE THIS MESSAGE?

*Artichokes used to annoy me, until I got to
thinking of their leaves as petticoats.*
—OLIVER WENDELL HOLMES

#56: REVERSALS

While many problems yield their solutions with a simple change of
viewpoint, others need complete reversal of direction. As a catalyst
for ideation, the principle of "reversal" has been responsible for
many new inventions. With this in mind, try to solve the following
problem:

HOLD A CLOTH NAPKIN AT TWO CORNERS AND TIE IT
INTO A KNOT. YOU'RE NOT ALLOWED TO LET GO OF
THE CORNERS ONCE YOU GRASP THEM.

*Small opportunities are often the beginning
of great enterprises.*
—DEMOSTHENES

#57: MAKING OPPORTUNITIES

Job-enrichment programs to improve the quality of work-life in the
office and the factory have been, by and large, disappointing, for
the challenge has been approached in a timorous and unimaginative
fashion. Actually, as Sidney X. Shore, consultant and trainer of
creativity/innovation management, states: "I know of no job, no
position, no profession which cannot grow and become more satisfy-

ing by looking for, recognizing, and above all by making opportunities and new advantages. Even the dullest, most routine job can be better if you look for and make opportunities on the job. . . . Every one of us who has made new opportunities (where none seemed to exist before) is aware of the excitement and pleasure such a life-style brings with it. . . . You grow, and others around you grow along with you. It is important in family living as well as in your organization and on your job."

Here's your chance to pull out all the stops and let your imagination soar as you think of all the ways a rather lowly job could be enriched with new opportunities and challenges.

ASSUME THAT YOUR JOB IS THAT OF A TRASH COLLECTOR IN A SUBURBAN COMMUNITY. THE DAILY ROUTINE HAS YOU RIDING THE TRASH TRUCK, STOPPING, WALKING TO THE REAR OF EACH HOUSE, EMPTYING THE REFUSE FROM RESIDENTS' GARBAGE BARRELS INTO YOUR OWN LARGER ONE, AND PERIODICALLY RETURNING TO THE TRUCK TO DUMP YOUR LOAD. IT'S A SMELLY JOB. IT'S NOT A TERRIBLY DIGNIFIED JOB, YOU FEEL. IT SURELY SEEMS LIKE A JOB WHERE YOU ARE NOT LIKELY TO MAKE OPPORTUNITIES! . . . OR IS IT?

PUT YOURSELF IN A GARBAGE COLLECTOR'S SHOES AND LIST AT LEAST 20 DIFFERENT OPPORTUNITIES HE CAN MAKE FOR HIMSELF, OPPORTUNITIES THAT WOULD GIVE HIM NEW ADVANTAGES.

*Humor is an affirmation of dignity, a
declaration of man's superiority to all that
befalls him.*
—ROMAIN GARY

#58: WACKY WORDIES

One of the most imaginative of visual wordplays is the rebus. A rebus is a kind of puzzle consisting of words, letters, numbers, signs, or objects, the combination and arrangement of which suggest phrases and sayings.

Sigmund Freud once remarked that we often become annoyed at having to stick to conventional rules, such as those that govern language usage. With rebus games we can break the rules and experience a sudden sense of comic relief. And the release that humor provides, together with a childlike playfulness of the mind and an iconoclastic "kicking over the traces" are some of the more effective ways to activate creative imagination.

CAN YOU DISCERN A FAMILIAR PHRASE, SAYING, CLICHE, OR NAME FROM EACH ARRANGEMENT OF LETTERS AND/OR DIGITS WHICH APPEARS ON THE FOLLOWING PAGES?

Examples
   Box 1a depicts the phrase "Just between you and me."
   Box 1b shows "Hitting below the belt."

Now try to decipher the rest of the "messages." After you have solved them, create a few of your own for your friends to puzzle over.

	a	b	c	d	e	f
1	you just me	belt hitting	head lo heels ve	V I O L E T s	B A E DUMR	agb
2	cry milk	r m u i i t	Symphon	pineapple cake	arrest you're	timing tim ing
3	O TV	night fly	S T I N K	injury + insult	r o rail d	my own heart a person
4	at the · of on	dothepe	wear long	strich groound	lu cky	the market

5					
worl	the x way	word YYY	search	go off coc	no ways it ways

6					
oholene	to e a r t h	ooo circus	1 at 3:46 and	late ⁿever	get a word in

7					
gone gone let be gone gone	a chance n	O MD BA PhD	wheather	world world world world	lo ose

8					
lines reading lines	chicken	y fireworks	L D Bridge	pace ̶k	danc t e s c etno

*Metaphor and simile are devices by which
our experience becomes refreshed, vivid, and
keen.*
—IRWIN EDMAN

#59: AS QUICK AS A WINK

Metaphors, similes, and analogies are some of the most potent tools for creativity. Aristotle stated that the ability to perceive metaphorically, to discern qualitative similarities between phenomena and objects, is a mark of genius. And the philosopher Ortega y Gasset declared: "The metaphor is perhaps one of man's most fruitful potentialities. Its efficacy verges on magic, and it seems a tool for creation which God forgot inside one of His creatures when He made him."

Here's another opportunity to develop this all-important ability.

THINK UP AN ORIGINAL SIMILE TO COMPLETE:

AS QUICK AS . . .

Example:
As quick as the lightning's flash.

Try to think up at least three original similes.

Now give it a twist. Instead of creating similes that mean "quick," create at least three similes that mean exactly the opposite, "slow." This frequently lends humor to your expression.

Example:
As quick as a blind man crossing the street.

Every real individual is a creative person.
This intrinsic creativity emerges, or is
expressed, when the person is free to use his
potentialities.
—CLARK E. MOUSTAKAS

60: VARIETIES OF CREATIVITY

People differ in how they are creative and how they express their creativity. They differ in their interests, values, and needs, in how they process reality, observations, problems, and how they arrive at new combinations of phenomena. Commonsense observation confirms this, but it does not explain why the differences exist.

Carl Gustav Jung offers a coherent scheme to help account for these divergent styles of creativity. His ingenious classification clarifies and conceptualizes our impressionistic and incidental observations about creative behavior.

There are eight types that Jung conceptualizes: • Extraverted Thinking • Introverted Thinking • Extraverted Feeling • Introverted Feeling • Extraverted Sensing • Introverted Sensing • Extraverted Intuitive • Introverted Intuitive.

Thinking, Feeling, Sensation, and Intuition are the functional types. Extraversion and Introversion are the attitudinal orientations.

In trying to understand personality as the origin of your creative style, the functional type offers the crucial key—it gives the personality its particular direction, its stamp and flavor, while the attitudinal orientation describes the direction of creative psychic energy.

According to Jung, there are two ways of perceiving: sensing, by which we become aware of things directly through our five senses, and intuition, by which we comprehend ideas and associations indirectly, through the unconscious. Although everyone makes use of both ways of perceiving, for a particular individual one always predominates and is preferred.

Two ways of judging are by thinking, a logical process that attempts to be objective and impersonal, and by feeling, a process of appreciation that is unabashedly subjective and personal.

Extravert, Introvert, or Somewhere Between

The introvert's main interests are in the inner world of personal or subjective events, concepts and ideas, and the extravert's are in the outer world of people and things. Therefore, when circumstances permit, the introvert prefers to direct perception and judgment upon ideas, whereas the extravert likes to direct both outwardly.

No one, of course, is exclusively one or the other. Most introverts can innovatively deal with the world about them when necessary, and extraverts can often deal effectively with ideas. But the introvert does his best work inside his head, in reflection, and the extravert does his best work externally, in action. In either case the preference for either introversion or extraversion remains, like a natural right- or left-handedness.

People usually underrate the value and strength of their primary functional and attitudinal direction. Because these are so natural to them, they erroneously believe that everyone else is also similarly capable, and so do not truly appreciate their unique personality, capacities, and gifts for expressing creativity. For example, creative extraverts generate lots of ideas about social behavior, whereas creative introverts can deal more effectively with new concepts, systems, and theories. One is creative about events "out there," while the other is creative about things "in here."

DISCOVER THE TYPE AND SOURCE OF YOUR CREATIVITY AS YOU UNIQUELY EXPERIENCE AND EXPRESS IT. CHECK TWELVE CHARACTERISTICS FROM THE LIST BELOW THAT DESCRIBE YOU BEST AS THE PERSONALITY YOU THINK YOU ARE.

Dominant	Dependable	Easygoing	Disciplined
Curious	Tactful	Modest	Imaginative
Energetic	Sensitive	Involved	Determined
Sincere	Analytical	Bold	Realistic
Quick	Committed	Diplomatic	Systematic
Confident	Enthusiastic	Practical	Warm
Efficient	Agreeable	Cheerful	Controlled
Perceptive	Adaptable	Patient	Decisive
Persevering	Considerate	Objective	Intellectual
Friendly	Organized	Independent	Logical

Observant	Mature	Stable	Conscientious
Understanding	Creative	Loyal	Soft-spoken
Stimulating	Factual	Quiet	Responsible
Painstaking	Reliable	Ingenious	Frank
Persistent	Cooperative	Open-minded	Sympathetic
Thorough	Tolerant	Serious-minded	Thoughtful
Clear thinking	Reserved	Idealistic	Intelligent
Forward-looking	Persuasive	Calm	

Work is only toil when it is the performance
of duties for which nature did not fit us, and
a congenial occupation is only serious play.
—ARCHIBALD LAMPMAN

#61: FROM A TO Z

In addition to providing you with another chance to increase your fluency and recall, this exercise gives you an indication of whether you have the particular interests, values, and motivations that predispose you to think and act creatively.

MAKE A LIST FROM A TO Z OF OCCUPATIONS OR CAREERS THAT YOU LIKE. THEN MAKE ANOTHER LIST, AGAIN IN ALPHABETICAL ORDER, OF THE OCCUPATIONS YOU DISLIKE.

Examples
Like: Auditor, buyer, carpenter .... zookeeper
Dislike: Army officer, butcher, cashier .... zoologist

*There are always twenty excellent reasons for
doing nothing for every one reason for
starting anything—especially if it has never
been done before.*
—PRINCE PHILLIP

#62: KILLER PHRASES

Most of us feel we are openminded, encouraging, and supportive of new ideas. This attitude, however, is seldom demonstrated. Indeed, it is safe to say that most people have a trigger-ready tendency to be overly critical when confronted with a new idea. They automatically feel a need to point out its shortcomings rather than its benefits or ways to make it work. Premature critical attitudes have caused the demise of countless valuable ideas.

This exercise is designed to make you aware of the negative reactions a creative notion frequently evokes. This awareness will enable you to formulate new, ingenious strategies for overcoming the many roadblocks your idea may encounter.

Part I
LIST AS MANY IDEA-SQUELCHING "KILLER-PHRASES" AS YOU CAN. WRITE DOWN THOSE YOU HAVE HEARD OR PERSONALLY EXPERIENCED AS WELL AS THOSE THAT MIGHT BE USED.

Examples
    It won't work . . .
    We haven't the time . . .
    We've tried that before . . .

NOW LIST YOUR OWN.

Part II
LIST AS MANY IDEA-SQUELCHING "SELF-KILLER-PHRASES" AS YOU CAN. LIST THOSE YOU MIGHT HAVE USED YOURSELF, OR OTHERS HAVE USED, OR MIGHT USE.

Examples
      This may not work, but . . .
      It isn't clear we need this, but . . .
      Would it hurt if we did . . .

NOW IT'S YOUR TURN.

> *To talk to someone who does not listen is*
> *enough to tense the devil.*
> —PEARL BAILEY

#63: CREATIVE LISTENING

Good listening is a creative act. It is crucial to effective communication. Yet, studies show that only about 10 percent of us listen well: many don't know how to, or don't want to, listen *creatively*.

It is generally assumed that in a dialog the speaker is more important than the listener. Certainly, both are vital. Yet, analysis of the communication process reveals that the listener is, indeed, the more significant link. The listener has the opportunity to *create* real communication just by the way he or she listens.

To most people, listening consists of trying to decipher, as fast as possible, the central point or gist of the speaker's message. The trouble is that this salient point is usually screened and frequently becomes distorted by the listener's preconceptions. Or there may be many subdivisions in a complex idea that can be missed. He tunes the speaker out as soon as he thinks he has grasped the gist of the message, then mentally prepares his own statement or rebuttal on the topic he *assumes* is being discussed.

The speaker has a thought or a mental image that he or she wants to convey. While he speaks, you listen. You cue on the key words based on your own associations, and then your mind fashions an *interpretation* of the message. If your interpretation creatively translated the speaker's words, your response will correspond to his meaning. If your conditioned reaction to a cue is not what the speaker intended, your response will not be addressed to his original meaning, and you will be talking on different wavelengths. The opportunity to learn and grow will be lost.

To avoid hearing in narrow translations based on your own preconceptions and biases, you need to process what you hear through a series of imaginative, alternative interpretations. Only after you have generated, sorted through, and weighed the possible responses are you ready to settle on one that most closely approximates what was really meant. Just as a scientist tests hypotheses, you must make assumptions about the speaker's meaning and "test" them as you pay close attention not only to what is said, but what lies behind the words.

Awareness of noncreative listening skills, coupled with a conscious effort at overcoming these deficiencies, goes a long way toward mastering the art of creative listening.

One of the best ways to test your own habits is to observe the bad, uncreative listening practices of others.

MAKE A DETAILED CHECKLIST OF ALL THE POOR AND IRRITATING LISTENING HABITS YOU HAVE OBSERVED IN OTHERS.

Examples

He constantly interrupts me while I'm talking—never lets me complete more than a couple of sentences before butting in.

When I'm talking, she finishes sentences for me.

> *The wise man will carefully conceal his*
> *superiority if he needs or wishes the*
> *cooperation of others to achieve success.*
> —FRANKLIN P. JONES

#64: DELEGATION

One of the biggest barriers to creative growth in organizational settings is the boss who fails to delegate responsibility and meaningful work. Not only does he or she limit his or her own effectiveness and creativity through nondelegation, but the subordinates will also lack the opportunity to develop and broaden their skills, motivation, initiative, judgment, and problem-solving abilities.

The first step toward correcting this rather endemic behavior pattern is to gain insight into why it occurs.

LIST ALL THE POSSIBLE REASONS YOU THINK OF WHY A BOSS OR A MANAGER DOES NOT DELEGATE AS MUCH WORK AS HE OR SHE SHOULD.

Examples
She has the feeling that if the job is going to be done right, she has to do it herself.
He is constantly harassed by unexpected emergencies, leaving no time for delegation.

NOW IT'S YOUR TURN.

> *The pace of events is so fast that unless we can find some way to keep our sights on tomorrow, we cannot expect to be in touch with today.*
> —DEAN RUSK

#65: FUTURE HEADLINES

Most of us are so deeply mired in here-and-now problems that we rarely think about the future, or if we do, the possible scenarios we project are laden with even greater dangers than we're experiencing at present.

The purpose of this game is to pull you out of the present and into a future frame of mind. It is an exercise of "imaginative realism" with a *positive* stance. Forecasting the future, verbalizing and discussing the posible *positive* developments, constitutes the first step toward influencing the days to come in a manner that would produce a less threatening and more desirable state of affairs.

CREATE FUTURE HEADLINES TO STORIES YOU
WOULD LIKE TO READ ABOUT IN YOUR NEWSPAPERS
WITHIN THE NEXT THIRTY YEARS.

This is a good game to play with others. After the participants
have listed their headlines, you can have a stimulating discussion
about whether or not each headline can indeed be anticipated within the thirty-year time frame. Since this is a game of exploration
rather than competition, there are no winners or losers. The purpose
is to focus attention on the future, and thus enable everyone to
become more pro-actively future oriented.

The power of imagination makes us infinite.
—JOHN MUIR

#66: STORY TIME

Dreaming, which is an act of pure imagination, attests that all of us
have profound creative powers. If these powers were available during our waking hours, we would be highly imaginative story-
tellers.
    This exercise is designed to narrow the gap between the poten-
tial you exhibit in your dreams and the realities of your everyday
life.

THROW A DIE TO SELECT A STIMULUS WORD FROM
EACH OF THE SIX CIRCLES. AFTER YOU HAVE YOUR
SIX WORDS, BUILD A LITTLE STORY AROUND THEM.

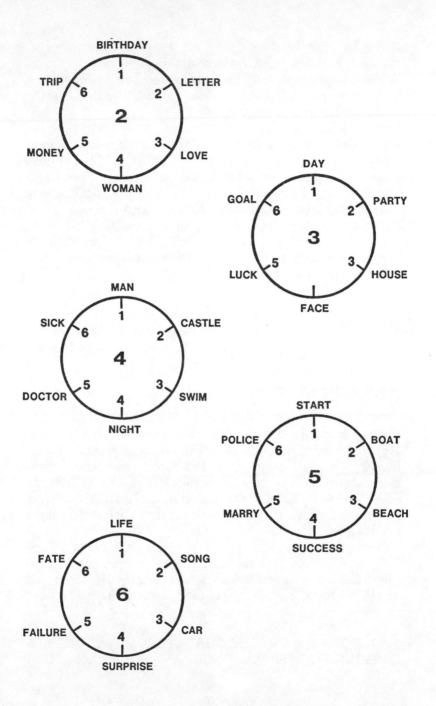

Examples

Accident, birthday, party, swim, boat, fate

It's no fun to have an *accident* on your *birthday*. For one thing you miss a *party*. You can't *swim* or go out in a *boat,* it might be *fate* but it sure is a bum trip.

Dream, love, party, swim, boat, car

Last night I had a *dream* that my *love* and I went to a beach *party.* I suggested to her we take a *swim* in the nude. We swam so far that somebody decided to send a *boat* after us. When we got back to the shore, a *car* was speeding away with all our clothes in it. To keep warm we had to hold each other real close.

Ghost, woman, party, man, woman, surprise

It might *surprise* you, but when a *man* and a *woman* decide to *marry,* the *party* is over. There isn't a *ghost* of a chance for them to live happily ever after.

Beaten paths are for beaten men.
—Eric Johnston

#67: WHAT IF . . .

So much in modern life is directing and controlling that it is hard to keep our imaginative powers alive. The ubiquitous pressures to conform force us to use commonplace and stereotyped modes of thinking, and it sometimes takes extraordinary measures to relax the deadly grip of compliance. One eminently useful technique for reawakening and liberating imagination is the "what would happen if" exercise.

Here, once again, you're asked to take on the role of a game designer. After you have created the items for the game, you and your friends can compete to see who will come up with the longest number of possible consequences to the unusual happenings and situations you imagined.

THINK OF AS MANY UNUSUAL CIRCUMSTANCES, SITUATIONS, OR HAPPENINGS AS YOU CAN THAT

WOULD TEST A PERSON'S CREATIVE IMAGINATION
AND INVENTIVENESS.

Examples
What would happen if . . .
   all people awakened tomorrow morning to find themselves twice
   as large?
   everyone could marry as many people as he or she wanted?

*If you train yourself to listen to your
intuition and to follow its bidding, you will
greatly increase your percentage of success in
life.*
—HAROLD SHERMAN

#68: FOLLOW YOUR HUNCHES

One of the most dramatic and useful forms of creative problem-solving is hunch or intuition. Many artists and scientists regard it as the key to creativity. Inventors of great note depended strongly on intuition for their creative insights. Thomas Edison, for example, was unusually prolific in generating useful hunches which when tested turned out to be right. He had learned to completely trust the feeling of certainty accompanying his intuitions. Similarly, Einstein said, "I believe in intuition and inspiration. . . . At times I feel certain while not knowing the reason." In most of his work, Einstein did not take the slow, painful, linear step-by-step process to solution, but relied instead on "feeling" his way to the right solution.

Intuitive ability is not restricted to geniuses or individuals with special talents. We all possess this capacity, but most of us have been conditioned by education and environment to neglect, repress, and distrust our intuitions. This is frequently implied in phrases such as "It was only a hunch," or, "I'm not going to play any hunches," or, "It's just a woman's intuition."

Since intuition, as a way of knowing, is crucial to creativity, you would do well to liberate and develop this latent ability. The following guidelines are presented to help you along.

•Determine first how strong your intuitive ability is. Start keeping a record of the intuitive hunches, flashes of insight, and images that come to you spontaneously and check later whether they had any validity.

•Motivate yourself to develop your intuitive abilities and believe in them.

•Set aside one time every day to tune in to your intuitive awareness and feelings.

•Learn to relax from physical and emotional stress. Tenseness prevents intuitive insights from rising to your conscious awareness.

•Meditative practices and reverie provide a direct pipeline to intuitive thinking. Excessive, unrelenting activity blocks intuitive awareness.

•Openness and sensitivity to both inner and outer reality enrich the fund of experiential information, which in turn expands intuitive knowing.

•Learning to trust the validity of your subjective experiences, impressions, and judgments helps you to develop trust and confidence in your intuitions.

•Do not confuse intuitive thinking with other modes of thought or emotion which are intimately personal, biased, wishful, or prejudicial. You must constantly analyze your thinking to separate genuine intuitive grains from emotional chaff.

•Realize that intuitive thinking is a perfectly normal function of the brain. It probably is not related to clairvoyance, mystical precognition, or similar phenomena.

•Intuition is used to its greatest advantage in solving problems that involve many complex, interrelated factors. When you have many variables, logical reasoning or quantitative techniques are frequently inadequate for synthesizing all the elements into a coherent whole. The intuitive mode, by comparison, utilizes multiple processing to carry out a work of creative synthesis.

The important thing is to recognize the value of the intuitive hunch when it occurs. Don't brush it aside or dimiss it as something irrational or unnatural. Use and act upon it, for it can be your springboard to successfully attaining your desired goals in life.

*Every realization of ideas contradictory to
established ruts of thought needs long and
thoughtful preparation.*
—ARNOLD BRECHT

#69: EVALUATING IDEAS

Many ideas are rejected, or become a "flash in the pan," because they are flawed. Frequently, sound evaluation would have corrected these defects. Yet it is amazing how many men and women still evaluate their ideas in a haphazard, nonsystematic fashion.

When you prepare a presentation of your idea without adequately evaluating it, you are almost sure to invite defeat. A few pointed questions could place you in a defensive position. You might then have to clutch randomly at supporting arguments and reasons. If, instead, you had thought through your idea, examined it, and subjected it to stringent evaluation, the chances are you would be able to work up a presentation that could withstand close scrutiny by others. To "sell" your idea, you have to demonstrate that you've thought it through.

This exercise is designed to give you a sound judgmental yardstick or evaluation checklist which you can apply to your ideas before presenting them to others.

CONSTRUCT A DETAILED SELF-QUESTIONING CHECKLIST YOU CAN APPLY TO EVALUATE THE WORTH OF YOUR IDEAS.

Examples
Does my idea fill a basic, existing need, or does the need have to be created?
What time, money, personnel, materials, or facilities are necessary to implement the idea?
Have I considered all the possible short-range and long-range benefits of the idea?
Whom do I have to convince of the value of the idea?

And so on.

A man has not seen a thing who has not felt it.
—HENRY DAVID THOREAU

#70: PINE CONE: SENSORY-AWARENESS ENHANCEMENT

The knowledge and pleasures that we receive from our environment come to us through two distinct modes of learning—reasoning and sensory involvement. Unfortunately, we most frequently learn through intellectual processes which follow the commonly accepted ideas of others rather than through our own immediate perceptions.

This exercise is designed specifically to nurture and promote reality that is sensed rather than reasoned. Such truth, beauty, and appreciation can be adjudged and measured only by one's own subjective and aesthetic standards. It can provide you with an invaluable opportunity for keener sensory responses; to see more, to feel more, to hear more, to taste and smell more intensely. It offers a means of understanding and appreciating that intellectual reasoning alone can never suffice, and it has a way of promoting self-discovery and enriching your life. Here is a symbol of your environment. It is a simple pine cone, but there is much more to any object in our environment than meets the eye. The basic principle of multisensory awareness applied here is applicable to any perceptive encounter.

This exercise does not attempt to give you an accumulation of facts about the pine cone to be deposited in your memory bank. Instead it attempts to develop your emotional abilities and increase your awareness and sensitivity. It has something for everyone. The exercise can be used as a game or conversation piece to enhance your pleasures, to overcome inhibitions, to transcend mere knowledge, to enrich imagination, to discover newness, to heighten your senses, and to make the world more accessible.

Specifically, this exercise is designed to:

• make your life more involved and intense

- encourage you to view experiences on a deeper and more personal level of understanding
- train you to utilize multisensory perception through your direct experiences of your relations, ideas, and feelings
- enhance your self-actualizing creativeness and your imagining and fantasizing capacities
- enhance the aesthetic quality of your experiences
- reawaken the affective processes and dimensions of your being, which enables you to incorporate that which you experience and encounter into your *total* being
- help you to derive inner, intensive, subjective, idiosyncratic knowledge that is not the result of the intellectual and rational processes alone, but is knowledge that is both sensed and reasoned

OBTAIN A PINE CONE AND PERCEIVE IT, NOT IN A CONVENTIONAL WAY WHICH SETS LIMITS TO YOUR AWARENESS, BUT CAREFULLY, DETECTING THE SENSATIONS THAT YOU ALONE ELICIT AFFECTIVELY FROM THE CONE; THE RECEPTIVE, EMOTIONAL QUALITIES. FIX YOUR MIND UPON DIRECT, IMMEDIATE, PERSONAL, AND EMOTIONAL RESPONSES.

What Does It Look Like?

Take a good look at your pine cone. What does this particular cone look like to *you*. Look directly at it and try to see its overall shape and the shape of its specific parts, its variations of color, texture, and design qualities. Turn it around and upside down and take a good look at it from different angles. Do not try to identify the various components in terms of the insights of others. Get in touch with your own reactions. Attempt to develop your capacity to see, sense, and experience in ways that deny conventions. Do not rationalize, but perceive and react personally and emotionally to the various stimuli. How do they affect you? How do they stimulate your emotions? Do they arouse calm? Do they please, displease, disgust, or soothe? Your reactions should evolve from your own experiences.

Sound Awareness

We too often have a tendency to perceive our environment with our eyes alone instead of using all our senses. Intense listening, for example, promotes another way of experiencing, understanding, and appreciating. Try rubbing the cone in the palm of your hand and listening to the sounds. With your nails, vigorously stroke the scales in one direction, then another. Does the sound change? Can you detect the difference? Do not just listen, but attempt to feel an emotional reaction. Focus on your inner self. What do the sounds do to you? Do they solicit joy and satisfaction or do they evoke unsympathetic responses? Make sounds by slapping the cone, tapping it with a pencil, dropping it on a table. Squeeze the cone and listen. Do it again and again. Break one of the scales, then several at the same time. How do these sounds affect you? Attempt to detect any echoing or vibrating qualities.

Not Touching But Feeling

When you touch an object you can learn about the texture of its surfaces. But even more importantly, you can also experience various feelings or "touch" sensations. Pick up the cone and try *not* to think of it objectively. Rely mostly on your sensory involvement. Experiment, explore, and through your own sense of touch arrive at your own convictions. How do the various surfaces of the cone feel to *you*? Are they appealing, irritating, perturbing, aggravating, or disturbing? As you handle the cone, what other sensations do you experience: warmth, coolness, dampness, dryness, weightlessness, perhaps a prickly feeling? Do not hesitate to pursue and voice your own sensations. Create new words and sounds that are compatible with each of your newfound feelings. Build a trust in yourself.

Smell Sensitivity

The process of smelling may not be as necessary to your well-being and survival as the other senses. Nevertheless, to neglect the development of smell awareness and sensitivity is to deny yourself of one of the avenues of becoming responsive and sensitive to your environment. In spite of the fact that your smell experiences are limited to an area of approximately two square inches in your nose, you are capable of developing the ability to experience several thousand different odors.

You can expand your smell responsiveness and discover new pleasures. Rely on the specifics of your experiences. Explore the pine cone with your sense of smell. Contemplate the effect that the smell of the cone has on you. Is it foul, spicy, fragrant, pleasing, repulsive? Fix your mind on your own imaginal responses. Wet the cone and experience the difference in odor. Burn part of the cone and discover a completely different sensation. A few whiffs can quickly saturate your smell sensors so that you can no longer respond sensitively to the cone. Give your nose a rest and return to your search a little later on.

Tasting And Savoring

Try for a direct acquaintance with the taste of the pine cone. Use a personal frame of reference so that what you taste is inspired by your awareness and feelings.

Although taste sensors are located solely in the mouth, this should not limit the possibilities of taste experiences. Taste is detected, for example, by various parts of the tongue, the soft palate, and the insides of the cheeks. There is an overlapping of taste sensations in these regions to be sure. The various regions, however, are not identical. One discerns sweetness more easily with the tip or front of the tongue, and quinine with the back of the tongue. The taste of a substance is also influenced by the size and temperature of the stimulus and the duration of exposure. Therefore, for maximum awareness experiment thoroughly.

Explore the wide range of taste by rolling one of the scales of the cone in your mouth slowly and deliberately so that it makes contact with various taste sensors. Contemplate and relish your tastes. Try tasting the scales after you have raised their temperature, soaked them in water, or chewed them for a while. The sensations that you experience from the taste of the cone are conditioned by the feeling of its texture as well as by its particular smell. Although taste sensations may seem almost unattainable on first encounter, continual effort will eventually pay off.

Cross and Mix Your Sensory Modes

At the beginning of this exercise you focused on each mode of sensory experience separately, attempting to sharpen your awareness through each of the sensory modes. Now train yourself to cross and mix your sensory modalities. This is not an easy task. Try not to distinguish between what you see, feel, hear, taste, and smell. Sensory crossover is a state in which there is no contradiction between sensorial responses. Such sensory mix embraces the total character of the pine cone and thereby enriches your awareness.

Try a few of the following imaginal experiences. They will be most helpful in establishing a sensory crossover and mix.

What does the texture of the pine cone smell like?
What does the color of the pine cone sound like?
What does the weight of the pine cone taste like?

Be sure to focus on what the texture smells like, the color sounds like, and the weight tastes like. Are you confused? Use your imagination. Create a sound for brown and stand by your conviction. Try not to concern yourself with authenticity.

> *Effort and achievement would exceed all expectations if the energies and imaginations of men could be freed of restrictions and restraints.*
> —CRAWFORD H. GREENEWALT

#71: KICK THAT BLOCK

Lack of creative receptivity and performance is not so much due to the absence of creative potential as it is to the various perceptual, cognitive, emotional, and environmental blocks and barriers. Once the inhibitors have been identified and removed, the immediate upsurge of creative output can be considerable.

This exercise is good to do in a group. When all participants have completed listing the blocks, each person takes turns verbalizing and discussing how and why each block inhibits creative problem-solving and what can be done to overcome it. The purpose of this is to provide everyone with a kind of *self-reclamation* journey that would open and release their creativity.

LIST THE BLOCKS AND BARRIERS THAT INHIBIT AND STIFLE CREATIVE PRODUCTION IN YOURSELF AND OTHERS.

Examples
   Lack of confidence in the ability to be creative
   Lack of motivation
   Lack of self-discipline
   Fear that idea will be stolen
   Fear of risk-taking

> *If you are not having problems, you are*
> *missing an opportunity for growth.*
> —THOMAS BLANDI

#72: MAKE A "BUG LIST"

All of us have problems, annoyances, peeves, and complaints of various kinds. Although we can do little or nothing about some of our problems, many of them can be solved creatively. There is a wonderful prayer that goes like this: "God grant me the serenity to accept the things I cannot change, the courage to change the things I can, and the wisdom to know the difference." Unfortunately, most people not only lack courage and wisdom, but they have never specifically thought about what precisely in life bothers them. And even if they are aware of a few things that cause discomfort or frustration, rare indeed are those men or women who do something effective or creative about them. You can be different.

This exercise is in two parts. First, take paper and pencil and list everything that bothers, annoys, or "bugs" you—specific problems and personal annoyances at home and at work, involving persons, objects, and events. The list should include those bugs that are common and shared by many, as well as far-out ones you consider to be your own. If you run out of problems and bugs in less than ten minutes, you're either a saint or extremely insensitive.

As the next step, list the problems or bugs you feel are most in need of creative solutions and write out the problem or problems you would like to tackle first. Writing down your problems enables you to crystallize your thoughts. It also commits you to do something about them and provides the needed motivational push.

Examples
   TV commercials
   People cracking knuckles
   Taking out the garbage

> *Without long, lovely moments spent in daydreams, life becomes an iron-ribbed sterile puffing machine.*
> —JOHN POWYS

#73: CREATIVE DAYDREAMING

One of the most powerful tools for bringing about a positive change in our personal lives is creative daydreaming, or fantasy making. There is increasing experimental evidence that what we visualize is what we get, and that we can deliberately program our own bio-computers with a set of self-fulfilling prophecies. We can imagine doing the work that we really enjoy; visualize the amount of money we'd like to make or the luxuries we'd like to obtain; or conceive any other goals that would promote our personal growth.

In order to properly "engineer" your future, you should picture yourself—as vividly as possible—the way you want to become, or with the comforts you want to attain. The important thing to remember is that you have to picture these desired objectives *as if you had already attained them.* Go over the details of these highly pleasant fantasy pictures several times. This procedure will indelibly impress them upon your memory. And these memory traces, or "engrams," as they are also called, will soon start influencing your everyday behavior toward the pictured goal of success.

While visualizing, you should be completely alone and undisturbed. Keep your eyes closed to help your imagination soar without inhibition. Many people find they obtain better results if they imagine themselves sitting before a large blank screen onto which they project the desired picture of themselves. Visual imagery is the predominant modality for daydreaming, and you have to make sure that your imagery is clear and sharp.

Some people first mentally relive some successful experience of the past to attain a positive, facilitative mood for daydreaming. When a mood of confidence and optimism has been attained, they then "cloak" it around whatever they want to accomplish.

Consultant/author Lew Miller advises you to build your scenario according to some *immediate* goal you want to attain. "Whatever it is, you write the script as it progresses, projecting yourself actively into as many successful, triumphant scenes as your imagination permits. Concentrate on it with burning desire. Then turn off the mental imagery and begin to act in daily life as if you already had achieved that goal. Turn on your little theater performance whenever a moment of solitude presents itself. Your faithful portrayal of the role you're playing will cause it to actualize in your life in direct proportion to the belief that you have in your own theatrical production."

Creative daydreaming is one of the most successful techniques for the attainment of a richer and fuller creative life. But, as is the case with almost any other useful technique, it must be practiced daily. Our attainments are limited by what we see as "possible." With daydreaming you can push back those limits and open up entirely new dimensions for your future.

Imagination is essential, and it comes first,
for without imagination we are aimless.
—C. N. Parkinson

#74: IMAGINE!

Having done the games and exercises, you have formulated many ideas about what creativity specifically means to you.

Now is your chance to express your knowledge.

CREATE SEVEN SENTENCES FOR WHICH THE SEVEN-LETTER WORD *IMAGINE* WOULD BE THE ACRONYM. ALL SENTENCES SHOULD REFLECT IN SOME WAY YOUR THOUGHTS ABOUT CREATIVE PROBLEM-SOLVING, IMAGINATION, RESOURCEFULNESS, AND INGENUITY.

Example

*I*deas should not be hoarded or hidden.

*M*any small solutions are necessary to solve big problems.

*A*ll people are created creative.

*G*ood ideas drive out bad ideas.

*I*nnovative ideas are resisted by older people.

*N*ever mind what others think—use your own judgment.

*E*njoy your fantasies—that's what they're for.

NOW IT'S YOUR TURN.

> *The creative consequences of man's imaginative strivings may never make him whole; but they constitute his deepest consolations and his greatest glories.*
> —ANTHONY STORR

#75: THE ULTIMATE

This exercise tests your visual acuity and speed of closure. Having conscientiously completed the preceding games and exercises, you should readily see what these lines represent.

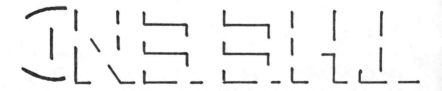

PART II

Examples and Answers

#1: HAVE A BALL!

Examples

(1) Head for finger puppet (2) Christmas tree ornaments (when painted and decorated) (3) Hang in fringe for low clearances (4) Clown nose (5) Target for slingshot, BB guns, .22 rifle, zip gun, spitballs (especially on water) (6) Juggle them (7) Gearshift knob (8) Roll down hill (9) Train dogs to retrieve (10) Wheels on toy automobile (11) Fish lure for big fish (12) Plug a hole (13) Hang on trees to frighten birds (14) Collect as a hobby (15) Make rattle for babies (16) Pulley for windowshade (17) Fill with lead and use for diving and retrieving (18) Window display (19) Stop up sink (20) Put on string for cat to play with (21) Cut up and cover eyes when sunbathing (22) Teach children to count (23) Construct mobile (24) False mumps (25) Hide narcotics (26) String as beads (27) Demonstrate structure (28) Costume for strippers (29) Decorate garden (30) Astronomical display

These are only some examples of the uses for balls. You probably came up with many others not listed here.

Devising alternative uses for common objects is not merely an academic exercise; it is continually demonstrated by those concerned about our environment. For example, among the countless varieties of manmade pollutants are the approximately 20 million discarded automobile and truck tires that litter our landscapes, highways, and dumps.

Many excellent and innovative ideas and solutions to this problem have already been developed. For example, Sidney X. Shore, publisher of the newsletter *Creativity in Action*, reported the idea of dumping discarded tires in offshore waters to form artificial "reefs." Fish and lobsters tend to gravitate to such protected habitats in the ocean waters, and fishing in these areas would yield rich harvests.

The Goodyear Company discovered that tires leave an insignificant amount of ash residue when used as part of the fuel supply to furnaces. The company also found that mixing ground-up tires with green-colored latex produces a type of "rubber turf" that would be an excellent surface for playgrounds.

Waste rubber could easily be added to asphalt paving to increase its toughness. The Environmental Protection Agency estimates that if new asphalt paving contained only 5 to 10 percent waste rubber, every tire discarded annually in the United States could be put to use.

All of the above uses, and others, have been tested and found practical and feasible. Unfortunately most of these ideas are presently not used, and the mountains of discarded tires grow larger each year, blighting our ecosystem.

There is no doubt that we can generate new and novel ideas to meet most of the challenges we are now facing and will face in the future. It is in the department of action and implementation that most of us fall short of the mark.

#2: MORE THAN MEETS THE EYE

Examples
(1) anvil (2) overpass pillar on highway (3) champagne glass (4) piano stool (5) tower with revolving restaurant (6) minute timer (7) propeller (8) chess game rook or castle (9) fruit holder (10) birdbath (11) chalice (12) rubber grommet (13) keyhole slot in door (14) extrusion die (15) two Pontiacs about to crash head-on (16) screw jack (17) arrowhead going into an object (18) two girls sitting back to back and holding parcels on their heads (19) balance wheel (20) modern version of the Illinois Central Railroad trademark (21) family insignia (22) filling a pen from an inkwell (23) island (24) smoke rising from an explosion (25) one-armed person pushing a button (26) old x-ray machine used by dentists (27) sexual intercourse (28) needlepoint pillow design (29) end table (30) ice cream dish (31) two spaceships, docking (32) hat for costume ball (33) stained-glass window (34) mirror (35) suction cup (36) swimming pool, new shape (37) chuck and piece of wood on a lathe (38) steer eating out of a food bin (39) saddle (40) floor polisher (41) clip-on paper clipboard (42) drawer pull (43) top spinning on a base (44) reflections of mountains in a lake (45) syringe filling a

bottle (46) design on ceramic tile (47) candleholder (48) flashlight (49) bottle, cute shape (50) paint scraper (51) doorknob (52) cross-section of a banister or hand railing (53) water fountain (54) reamer (55) bung puller (56) molehill (57) eyewash cup (58) cave (59) staircase pole (60) UFO (61) shock absorber (62) coffee table (63) two Eskimos rubbing noses (64) skull (65) cross-section of an automobile wheel, tire rim (66) Buddha figure (67) radar cone (68) bath or shower faucet handle (69) top half of a half-buried anchor (70) spun aluminum dish on a lathe (71) flower (72) shower head (73) device for removing snow from a car's windshield (74) streetlight.

Have another look at the drawing, and with the list above see if you can "see" some of these items that you might not have visualized before. Chances are that you will find even more to see in this very simple sketch.

#3: PAIRING UP

Examples
(1) Socks (2) Stockings (3) Bookends (4) Salt and pepper shakers (5) Stereo speakers (6) Dumbbells (7) Turn signals (8) Running lights (9) Twin beds (10) Bedside tables (11) Ping Pong paddles (12) Skis (13) Skates (14) Swim fins (15) Falsies (16) Breasts (17) Nipples (18) Eyes (19) Ears (20) Nostrils (21) Hands (22) Feet (23) Siamese twins (24) Oars (25) Crutches (26) Lungs (27) Handcuffs (28) Cufflinks (29) Legs (30) Married couples (31) Yoke of oxen (32) Eyebrows (33) Lips (34) Buttocks (35) Testicles (36) Andirons (37) Candlesticks (38) Doorknobs (39) Eyeglasses (40) Earmuffs (41) Lovebirds (42) Window shutters (43) Bicycle wheels. And so on.

#4: HOW OB(LI)VIOUS I

Answers
   1. One hour. The alarm would go off at 9 that night.

2. All 11 months.
3. The beggar is the woman's sister.
4. He is still living.
5. Yes.
6. If you throw it straight up in the air.
7. Hold the egg up and drop it from a height of 6 feet. It will drop 5 feet without breaking. After that you will need to clean up the mess.
8. The 2 fathers and 2 sons were: a son, his father, and his father's father.
9. Only once. After the first time, you're subtracting from 22, then 20, and so on.
10. One sizable haystack.
11. 12.
12. Two girlfriends at the same time: 3 admission tickets. One girlfriend twice: 4 tickets.
13. Five apples, naturally.
14. He was lying. No one knew Christ was coming in 459 years.
15. If you're governed by the profit motive, you'd choose half a truckload of dimes, since they're smaller and worth twice as much.
16. 9.
17. The spare tire was flat.
18. Suicide.
19. They all could take turns and sit on your lap. You certainly couldn't accomplish that.
20. Her hat was hung over the end of the gun.

#5: TANTALIZING TANS

Examples

1 2 3

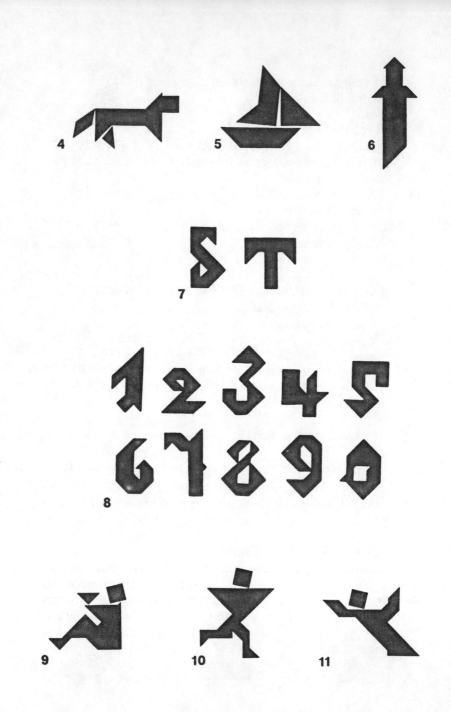

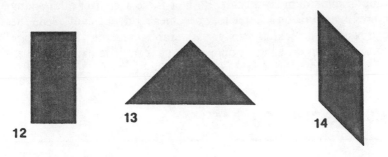

12   13   14

#6: CLOSE ASSOCIATES

Part I

Answers
(1) bank (2) egg (3) tight (4) light (5) escape (6) record (7) sheep
(8) plug (9) dumb (10) line (11) trap (12) flat (13) goose (14) wise
(15) double (16) apple (17) night (18) hot (19) tip (20) check (21)
out (22) field (23) ring (24) over (25) peter

Part II

Answers
(1) jack (2) ant (3) hum (4) fat (5) cat (6) ball (7) pal (8) off

One of the major attributes of successful inventors is the ability
to see correspondences or similarities not immediately apparent to
others. What inventors generally do is to bring the operating principles, or associative elements, of a device from one field into con-
tiguity with an entirely different one.

Although there have been innumerable examples of associative
combinations over the centuries, a very contemporary example will
serve; it's a very popular child's stroller. Formerly, baby strollers
were built on the baby carriage principle. They were almost invariably heavy, awkward, and impossible to load into buses, planes, and
subcompact automobiles. Not long ago a team of inventors took
note of the problems and redesigned the baby stroller, using as
models "things that fold for carrying" like the umbrella and the

tubular aluminum lawn chair. Both of these are, after all, nothing more than fabric on a frame that becomes rigid when unfolded. The end result was a folding stroller with umbrella handles light enough to be transported hanging on a person's arm. The name was well chosen to reflect the synthesis. They called it "The Umbroller."

#7: DOODLES GAME

1. Upside-down balloon
   A sperm cell listening to a different drummer
   A balloon following an encounter with a child's perfectly aimed stone
   Hair-sprayed pigtail
   An idea looking for a home
   An orange with an umbilical cord
   A hair-raising experience
2. Smokestack with handles
   Giant coffeepot
   A husband and wife coffee cup
   Back view of little girl with long hair and big glasses
   Traveling beehive
   Goodyear blimp behind a skyscraper
   Coffeepot for the ambidexterous
   Three Mile Island atomic coffeepot
   Nun listening to a stereo
3. Tall building with air-conditioning unit on top
   A man wishing he had called a chimneysweep
   Two little cats sleeping in a pipe
   Historic moment: a climber is reaching the top of Man-made Mountain
   Toes sticking out of a short blanket
   Two ants about to mate above a firecracker
   Bottom view of a diving board before a flatfooted person takes a dive
   Friendly encounter of two caterpillars
4. Portholes
   A woman with a hoop skirt standing on a glass floor

A bucket of water and an anxious, thirsty boy
Nearsighted "Alien"
Bottom view of a fat person leaping off a roof of a building
John Glenn coming down from orbit with a hangover
Two footprints in a mudhole
"Gee, I'm sleepy."
A fat man doing a yoga headstand
Bottom view of a person falling down a well
Helmet of an underwater diver

5. Sun and moon
Mother marble to baby marble: "You can do it, roll to me!"
Greasy soup
Two-yoke egg
Portholes in a submarine
Three circles of different sizes
Golf ball and a hole

6. Rabbit ears
The start of a banana race
"My point and your point might be equal, but they don't meet."
Dracula's incisor teeth
Part of Bat Man's cape
A pianist running from the stage
The beak of a talkative bird
Pair of scissors that won't close
"I see your good points, what about the bad?"

7. Breast
"I don't need to shave yet, my chin is so clean, see!"
Top view of fat person with arms folded in back
Top view of boy holding a beach ball
Rear view of girl with a bun
A fly asleep on a golfball
Skier buried in snow, only the cap is visible
Toiletseat
Christmas wreath

8. Battery
Abe Lincoln taking a shower

Elephant balancing act
Elephant with a splinter in his foot
Tailpipe of a VW
Elephant foot with an outgrown toenail
Smokestack
Midget puppet in a stovetop hat
Abe Lincoln in a voting booth

#8: DIFFERENT CIRCLES

Examples

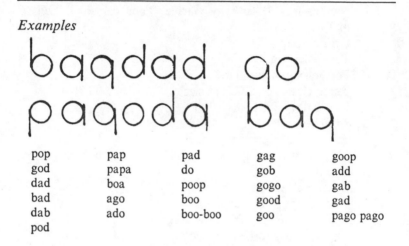

pop	pap	pad	gag	goop
god	papa	do	gob	add
dad	boa	poop	gogo	gab
bad	ago	boo	good	gad
dab	ado	boo-boo	goo	pago pago
pod				

#9: MATTER OF SEMANTICS

Answers

1. felicitous—appropriate
2. jovial—hearty
3. tenacity—persistence
4. alacrity—briskness
5. simulate—feign
6. recondite—abstruse
7. frustrate—thwart
8. emanate—issue
9. bombastic—high-flown
10. palliate—mitigate
11. theory—hypothesis
12. stricture—criticism
13. expound—interpret
14. equivocal—ambiguous

15. mien—bearing
16. fidelity—loyalty
17. sagacious—shrewd
18. refractory—stubborn
19. obdurate—unfeeling
20. tentative—experimental
21. esoteric—profound
22. relegate—consign
23. ephemeral—transitory
24. cynical—sneering
25. sentient—sensitive
26. explicit—definite
27. amorphous—formless
28. dissident—differing
29. perspicacity—discernment
30. fortitude—courage

#10: CELEBRATION

Answer

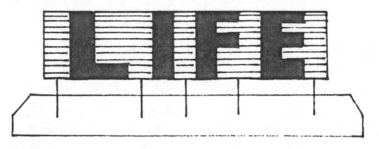

#11: CREATE A GAME

Examples
1. The restaurant Metropol often features name bands.
2. Shaved ice goes best with this drink.
3. Sam bathes at least twice a week in the ocean.
4. Let racketeers profit from this if they wish, you shouldn't.
5. Do you remember the song Bing often sang?
6. You shouldn't poke Ralph in the ribs.
7. I cannot wrest linguistic meaning out of this.
8. After the gangster was shot, Putnam received a promotion.

9. You have to clean this rug by evening, before the guests arrive.
10. Put tapes in the can as tapes deteriorate in the open air.
11. Ten Nishapurians decided to return home and visit the birthplace of Omar Khayyám.
12. The dumb ox ingloriously tried to escape.
13. Put this bad mint on the tray so the hostess can see it.
14. The singer hit a high la, crossed her legs, and reached the high do.
15. You'll have to log olfactometer readings into this book.
16. New Jersey's crab blends well with other seafood.
17. The very popular Cher yakked too much on her last TV show.
18. The refrain consists of sol, do, mi, re, si, re, do, mi notes.

#12: LOOSE STRINGS

Answers

Psychologist Norman R. Maier indicates that most solutions to this problem fall into four broad categories, and each category requires a switch in perceptual viewpoint.

Category A: If you see the problem in terms of "inadequate reach," then the solutions involve extending your reach by means of a cane, umbrella, stick, pole, or some other object with a handle.

Category B: If you perceive the problem as "the strings are too short," then your solutions call for ways to extend the length of the strings, for example, tying another string, a belt, windowshade cord, ruler, or other object to them.

Category C: If you feel that "one string won't stay in the middle while I reach for the other," your solutions involve ways to tie one string down in the center, either to a chair, a suitcase, television, or any other object that you can readily move around.

Category D: If you perceive the problem as "the second string won't come to me while I'm holding the first," then your solutions could involve utilizing a fan, opening windows or doors to create a breeze, tying magnets to the strings, or tying a ring, key, or some other object to the string and swinging it like a pendulum.

If your solutions entailed all four categories, you're displaying extraordinary versatility and flexibility in your thinking.

#13: JOINED TOGETHER

This design can be copied easily, accurately, and elegantly in less than 40 seconds.

One step-by-step approach is as follows:

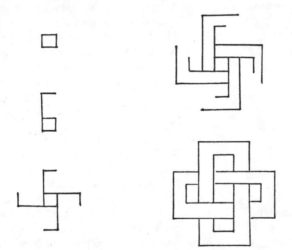

Another imaginative solution occurs when you recognize the pattern as being made up of four identical parts. Drawing them one after another and rotating each successive part 90 degrees makes a speedy reproduction, like this:

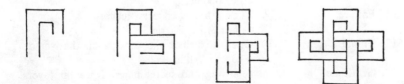

Some people tape two pencils together and zip through to a speedy solution.

#.14: APHORISTIC DEFINITIONS

Examples

1. Advertising — The science of arresting the human intelligence long enough to get money from it. —Stephen Leacock

2. Argument — A sure sign of conversation gone sour. —Dagobert D. Runes

3. Block — The distance between some people's ears.

4. Bore — A person who talks when you wish him to listen. —Ambrose Bierce
   A fellow who opens his mouth and puts his feats in it. —Henry Ford
   A man who deprives you of solitude without providing you with company. —Gian Vincenzo Gravino

5. Conceit — Self-respect in one whom we dislike. —Ambrose Bierce

6. Cynic — A man who knows the price of everything, and the value of nothing. —Oscar Wilde

7. Depression — A period when you can't spend money you don't have.

8. Doctor — Someone who acts like a humanitarian and charges like a TV repairman. —Henry D. Spalding

9. Envy — The sincerest form of flattery. —Churton Collins

10. Executive — A person who can, without the facts, make quick decisions that occasionally are right.
    A person who earns his living by the work of other people.

11. Failure — The path of least persistence. —James M. Barrie

12. Friend — One who dislikes the same people that you do. —Oscar Wilde

13. Gratitude — A strong and secret hope of greater favors. —La Rochefoucauld

118

14. Happiness	A delicate balance between what one is and what one has. —J. H. Denison
15. Initiative	Doing the right thing without being told. —Elbert Hubbard
16. Life	One long process of getting tired. —Samuel Butler
17. Luxury	Something you don't really need and can't do without.
18. Marriage	A noose often endured around the neck, but seldom endured around the feet. —Henry S. Haskins
19. Pessimist	One who, when he has the choice of two evils, chooses both. —Oscar Wilde
20. Politician	A fellow who shakes your hand before the election and shakes you after the election.
21. Procrastination	The art of keeping up with yesterday. —Don Marquis
22. Progress	The exchange of one nuisance for another nuisance. —Havelock Ellis
23. Reality	A poor substitute for imagination. —Dagobert D. Runes
24. Self-Evident	Evident to one's self and to nobody else. —Ambrose Bierce
25. Self-Respect	The secure feeling that no one, as yet, is suspicious. —H. L. Mencken
26. Storyteller	A person who has a good memory and hopes other people haven't. —Irwin S. Cobb

#15: SIGHTWORDS

Examples

   G AP

PEOPLE

NDER
U

see

BLOWOUT

$UÇÇE$$

TIE

delicate

PASTOR

mountain

SLOPE

EiSH

frac
tion

FOGGY

camel

SQUEEZE

N♪♫TE♪

#16: AROUND THE CIRCLE

Examples

Expensive (2) Round (9)

Gold ring, pearl, gold coin, antique clock, crystal bowl, gold bracelet

Yellow (1) Heavy (6)

Sun, ton of corn, 500-pound block of butter, yellow house, maple tree in the fall, gold in Fort Knox

Expensive (2) Durable (12)

Rolls-Royce, diamonds, platinum, gold, silver, iridium, a loyal wife

Useful (5) Elastic (8)

Girdle, rubber bands, tourniquet, bra, rubber gloves, the American dollar

Heavy (6) Round (9)

Barrel of wine, water tower, pipe filled with concrete, lead ball, tub of water, telephone pole, marble column, obese person, farm tractor tires, turbine engine

#17: SQUARES APLENTY

Answer: 30 squares.

Once you saw beyond the obvious answer—16, or perhaps 17 (if you counted the square that contains the smaller ones), you were on your way to solving the problem.

There are two important factors of creative problem-solving here. The first is the repressive notion of exclusivity—the idea that once you've identified a unit it cannot be used again as part of a larger unit. There are, of course, squares within squares.

The other quality is persistence. Effective problem-solving is seldom done in a hurry.

#18: TELL ME A STORY

Example: An old trombone. A broken doll.

A man was very fond of playing his trombone and had, prior to marriage, played regularly with the local band. His wife hated the instrument and used to make a scene whenever he tried to practice.

The wife, however, had a habit that annoyed her husband. Although a grown woman, she still used to play almost daily with a big doll. Her husband teased her because of this childish habit and one day he broke the doll.

To retain marital harmony they agreed to give up their respective "hobbies" and took the trombone and the broken doll to the attic. From that time on, however, their marriage deteriorated to a point at which they contemplated divorce.

One Sunday the wife decided to clean out the attic and ran across the old trombone and the broken doll. She suddenly realized that here was the cause of all their troubles. She took them down to the livingroom and the couple made up.

The husband became such a good musician that he gave up his dull job and started to play with a band that traveled a lot. She started designing dolls and was so successful that she began her own doll factory.

Some people feel inhibited about telling or writing stories because they compare it to masterful and polished writing. This is ridiculous. As W. Somerset Maugham pointed out, "The four greatest novelists the world has ever known, Balzac, Dickens, Tolstoy and Dostoyevsky, wrote their respective languages very indifferently. It proves that if you can tell stories, create characters, devise incidents, and if you have sincerity and passion, it doesn't matter a damn how you write."

#19: THE CONSCIENTIOUS DRIVER

Answer: 26,062. 55 miles per hour

Since it would be clearly impossible for the first digit of 25,952 to change in 2 hours, 2 would have to remain the first and last digit of the new number. The second and fourth digit could not change to more than 6. If the middle digit was 2 or 1, then the car would have traveled 310 or 210 miles in 2 hours. Since Aunt Nellie was a conscientious driver, the middle digit would have to be 0, and the car traveled 55 miles per hour, which is the speed limit on most highways

#20: CRAZY BUT NOT STUPID

Answer

The patient said, "You could take one lug off of each of the other wheels and then drive to town to replace the lugs." The man was truly amazed and asked, "If you're so smart, how come you're in there and I'm out here?" The reply was, "I may be a little crazy, but I'm not stupid."

Among the precepts most of us have learned which are not true is that all the lug bolts on an auto wheel must be in place in order to drive a car.

As a matter of fact, most mechanical devices are "overengineered." They can be subjected—when necessary—to unusual stress for short periods of time without serious consequences. Basic operational rules can be suspended when circumstances warrant. Being able to act in a nonconforming manner for a specific purpose is part of creative behavior.

#21: TUESDAY'S TRANSACTIONS

Examples

On Mondays, businessmen are still in a "weekend frame of mind" and don't begin functioning well until Tuesday.

Businessmen travel on Mondays to produce Tuesdays' deals.

Tuesdays' deals are actually Friday and Monday transactions not tallied until Tuesday.

Monday is the day for preparing documents reflecting deals agreed to in the past week. They are signed on Tuesdays.

Weather bureau records show that Tuesdays are sunny more often than any other day of the week, and are thus conducive to successfully concluding business transactions.

Loose ends left over from the previous week are completed on Mondays, leaving Tuesdays free for business deals.

Mondays are used for doing the groundwork for Tuesdays' transactions.

Business people take longer lunch hours on Tuesdays to conduct their business and thus conclude a greater number of deals.

Tuesday is preferred because it is considered a "lucky" day.

Businessmen's energy levels peak on Tuesdays, making them more aggressively determined to successfully conclude their business objectives.

#22: THE MAGIC BOX

Answers

32

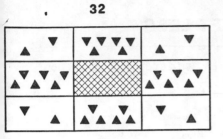

26

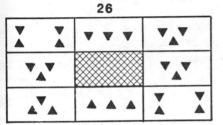

24

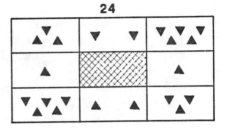

22

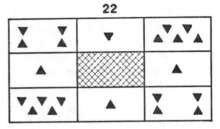

#23: IDEA

Examples

I dance every afternoon.
It doesn't eliminate air.
Indecision delays economic achievement.
Italy, Denmark, England agree.
Iron deposits estimated adequate.
If Daddy ever agrees?
Ireland denies every accusation.
Ingrid does everything attractively.
Intentions determine every action.
Ivan discourages every agreement.

#24: ADD MORE TO GET LESS

The most obvious solution is XX | with added line as fraction bar, XX/l

Other solutions

XX+ Twenty plus nothing is twenty.

XX|— When this is turned sideways it becomes
X two tens over one,
X̲ which is twenty.
I

The solutions shown above are just some involving the use of a *straight line*. However, the problem statement was: "Add one line . . ." Therefore, with no stipulation as to the shape of the line, it would be an *unwarranted assumption* to try to solve this problem with only *straight lines*.

As long as you produce a line with just one sweep of the pen, without lifting it from the paper, that constitutes "one line." With this in mind, the following solutions are also permissible:

XX ⅍ A proofreader's deletion mark

X̶X̶Ⱦ The line cuts XX | into twenty segments.

XX√⌐ Twenty times square root of one is twenty.

[XX] Twenty in a box

Other possibilities X̶X̶T̶ Twenty line segments

X̶X̶⌐ This makes ∨ and ∨ ⌐

above the line ⌐ ∨ and ∨ and

below the line (upside down).

#25: 'PUN MY WORD

Examples

Florist—We rest on our laurels.
Upholsterer—I'm as sharp as a tack.
Farmer—My business is growing.
Electrician—I get a charge out of my business.
Carpenter—We nail it down.
Shoemaker—We save soles.
Garbage Collector—My business is picking up.
Fireman—Business is getting hot.
Preacher—Sin is our most important product.
IRS clerk—Things just don't add up.
Dairy Farmer—Our work is no bull.
Toiletseat Manufacturer—Born in Barrie, raised everywhere.
Astronomer—My business is looking up.
Basketball Player—Things are really jumping.
Surgeon—I'm a regular cutup.
Mortician—I bury others' mistakes.
Miller—I really grind it out.
Dynamite Salesman—My business is booming.
Deep-sea Diver—Business is really down.
Banker—We're in the money.
Pharmacist—We dispense with accuracy.

#26: COIN SHIFT

Answers

1. With your left index finger press firmly on the dime. With the right index finger (or two fingers), slide the right-hand quarter to the right, then strike firmly against the dime. The left-hand quarter will spring aside. Move the right-hand quarter into the exposed space.

2. Press your fingers tightly on the dime and the right-hand quarter. Blow at the left-hand quarter and it'll move aside.

3. Hold the dime and the right-hand quarter firmly in place. With your left knee lift the right-hand side of the table sufficiently for the left-hand quarter to slide away.

4. Place the left-hand quarter on a piece of paper so half of it extends beyond it. Then move the paper with quarter to the left.

#27: SUCCESS AND FAILURE

Examples

S—Stick-to-itiveness, skill, synergy, strength, soundness, solidity

U—Uprightness, unflappability, uniqueness, unity, usefulness, unsuspiciousness

C—Charisma, cash, concentration, considerateness, creativity, character

C—Credibility, cooperativeness, coolheadedness, constancy, confidence, clout

E—Experience, excellence, earnestness, effectiveness, endurance, empathy

S—Surefootedness, study, serenity, self-realization, security, support

S—Serendipity, sharp-sightedness, specialization, staunchness, sobriety, showmanship

F—Fussiness, frustration, foolishness, fanaticism, falseness, frivolity

A—Aimlessness, arrogance, artificiality, abstruseness, automatism, antagonism

I—Isolation, irresoluteness, intolerance, insolence, inflexibility, ineptitude

L—Loafing, lucklessness, low-mindedness, lethargy, ludicrousness, listlessness

U—Untimeliness, unreadiness, unapproachableness, unconcernedness, underemployment, upstartness

R—Rashness, revengefulness, rigidity, resignation, reclusiveness, randomness

E—Envy, exhibitionism, extremism, egocentricity, emptyheadedness, escapism

#28: DON'T FENCE ME IN

Answers

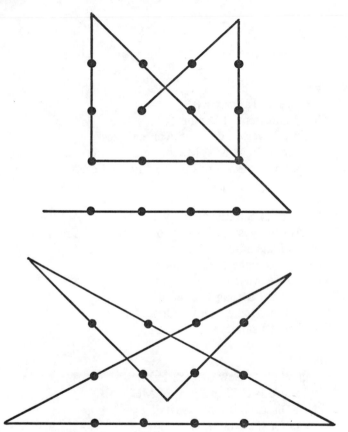

#29: HUMOROUS TITLES

Examples
Nixon
   "Let Me Make It Perfectly Erased"
   "Great Fairy Tales of the White House"

"Water Over the Gate"
"Kicking It Around"
"More Fascinating Facts About My White House Years"
"How to Live Well Writing Memoirs, and Other True Confessions"

Nixon & Kissinger
"Our Secret Missions"

Kissinger
"In Praise of Taller Girls"
"The Quintessential Diplomat"
"Politics, Power, and Other Aphrodisiacs"
"The Three Great M's: Machiavelli, Metternich, and Me"
"Compromising Positions in the Middle East"

Carter
"The Natural Superiority of Wives"
"The Advantages and Pitfalls of On-the-Job Training"
"How to Flagellate the Tush"
"There's No Place Like Home"
"You Can Always Get a High from Jogging"
"How to Be a Strong Leader"
"My Confidence and Other Crises"
"SALT and Peanuts"

Parton
"Seven Ways to Sew Stretch Fabrics"
"My Future Is Still in Front of Me"
"How I Discovered Antigravity"
"Thanks for the Mammories"

#30: WORD CHANGE

Answers
1. Care 2. Mare 3. Mire 4. Mine 5. Mind
1. Write 2. White 3. Whine 4. Thine 5. Think

#31: LIKE/UNLIKE

Examples: Part I
    Straight lines ZXTNKHE
    Horizontal lines ZTHE
    Parallel lines ZNHE
    Open at the top and bottom XNKH
    Open at the right ZXTSKEC
    Open at the left ZXSTJ
    Open at the top XNKH
    Open at the bottom XNKH
    Even-numbered letters in alphabetical sequence ZXTNJHDB
    Odd-numbered letters in alphabetical sequence SKEC

Examples: Part II
    Z is the only letter with 2 parallel horizontal lines.
    Z is the only letter either at the beginning or the end of the alphabet.
    X is the only letter with 2 diagonal straight lines.
    X is the only letter open on all sides.
    T is the only letter containing 1 single horizontal line.
    T has the only numerical spot divisible by 10.
    S is the only curved-line letter that can be turned upside down and still remain the original letter.
    S is the only letter containing two opposite curved lines.
    N is the only letter that turned sideways would look like the last letter (" Z ").
    N is the only letter that is 5 letters away from the letter preceding it (" S ").
    K is the only letter that precedes two letters that make up a word (HE).
    K is the only letter that contains 1 straight and 2 diagonal lines.

H is the only letter that contains 2 vertical and 1 horizontal line.

H is the only letter that phonetically is spelled with "a" (āch).

E is the only letter that has 2 open areas at the right.

E is the only letter that has 3 horizontal straight lines.

D is the only letter that contains 1 closed half-circle.

D is the only letter that contains 1 completely enclosed space.

C is the only open single-curved letter.

C is the only letter that stands for the first note in the scale of C major.

B is the only one that has two completely enclosed spaces.

B is the only letter that looks like a numeral (3) when the vertical straight line is removed.

J is the only letter that hangs under the line it is written on.

#32: IN OTHER WORDS

Examples
Irrational, ill-advised, erroneous, ill-considered, incorrect, ludicrous, nonsensical, ridiculous, stupid, absurd, unreasonable, wild, senseless, preposterous, mistaken, ill-judged, extravagant, farcical, grotesque, queer, awkward, muddled, egregious, unintelligent, brainless, addlepated, fatheaded, rattlebrained, nitwitted, shortsighted, thick-skulled, nutty, heavy, obtuse, stolid, dotish, asinine, silly, incompetent, simplistic, puerile, fatuous, idiotic, driveling, frivolous, trifling, inept, imbecilic, moronic, blatant, babbling, vacant, sottish, bovine, apish, insensate, maudlin, unwise, indiscreet, injudicious, improper, clumsy, bungling, unfit, ass backwards, basket case, birdbrain, blockhead, dimwitted, dumb bunny, dumbo, goofy, goop, clod, klutz, hot air, jerky, jay, knucklehead, lug, lunkhead, missing some buttons, monkeyshines, nudnik, numb, numbhead, pinheaded, square, stupe, sucker, tack head, tinhorn, unscrewed, X-double minus, zilch, zonk

#33: A PERFECT MATCH

Answers

1.

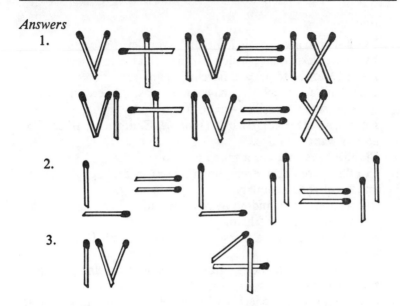

2.

3.

4. Simply walk around to the other side of the table. Or turn the book upside down.

5.

6.

7.

#34: WHAT'S GOOD ABOUT IT?

Examples

I've lasted longer in this job than anyone ever expected.

I've gotten experience which will be valuable in a new job.

I really wanted to get a different job anyway.

I can land a new job that pays me at least 25 percent more.

My boss was impossible—glad to be rid of him/her.

I can now move to Arizona (Florida, California), where I've always wanted to live.

I'll now have time for a much needed vacation.

I've discovered new strengths in myself in dealing with crises, and I feel good about that.

My relatives are standing by me with aid and comfort, which I never expected from them.

I would have had a nervous breakdown had I stayed any longer.

I can get enough money from unemployment to give me a breathing spell.

My severance pay together with my new job will put me ahead financially.

I begin to know who my true friends are.

I now have time to sort things out, examine and clarify what I really want from life.

I can find a more challenging job, better suited to my talents and interests.

I won't have to pay so much income tax.

I can now go into business on my own—something I've always wanted.

My mate will now get the opportunity to have a career of his/her own.

I have the time now to fix up the house.

I can now engage in more sports and recreational activities.

As with any new technique, it takes practice to become adept at it. Set aside 15 to 20 minutes, once a week. Write down as simply as you can a difficult situation of your own, or of someone close to you. Ask the question "What's Good About It?" . . . and start writing.

#35: OVALATION

Examples

Also
Mirror, Kleenex box opening, ashtray, face, hanging lampshade, vase, sardine can, sign, spoon, eyecup, teabag can, lemon, egg, basket, window, swimming pool, toiletseat, White House office, ladybug. (Remember, any circular shape seen from an angle appears as an oval shape.)

#36: BOATRIDE

Examples
    A Practical Education
    A Matter of Priorities
    A Matter of Perspective
    A Little Learning . . .
    Think and Swim
    Who's Sorry Now?
    First Things First
    Pedant's Perplexity
    Different Strokes
    Point, Counter Point
    Drone's Drown
    Eggheads Can't Float
    Grammarian's Last Gaff
    Pedant's Pride

#37: NUMBERS GAMES

Answers

1.
16	2	3	13	= 34
5	11	10	8	= 34
9	7	6	12	= 34
4	14	15	1	= 34
= 34	= 34	= 34	= 34	= 34

2. The difference between our ages is still 32 years, so I must be 32 if my mother is twice as old.
3. They have the same sums. If you look closer and compare just a few digits, e.g., nine 1's match one 9, eight 2's match two 8's, it soon becomes apparent that the sums are equal.
4. 99 9/9
5. 99 99/99
6.
```
   888
    88
     8
     8
     8
  ----
  1000
```
7. $7 + 415 + 689 = 1111$, or $74 + 56 + 981 = 1111$, and so on
8. $111 - 11 = 100$
   $(5 \times 5 \times 5) - (5 \times 5) = 100$
   $(5 + 5 + 5 + 5) \times 5 = 100$
   $(5 \times 5) (5 - [5 \div 5]) = 100$
9. 8
   $(7 \times 7 = 49)$
   $(4 \times 9 = 36)$
   $(3 \times 6 = 18)$
   $(1 \times 8 = 8)$
10. 4 pears. 7 pears.

#38: THUMBPRINT DRAWINGS

Examples

#39: SELECTIVE DIAGNOSTIC INDICATOR

With such a powerful diagnostic tool at your disposal, it is hard to say to what degree you will endear yourself to professionals in the mental health and behavioral sciences fields, but you can drop the phrases into virtually any conversation at parties and they will have a ring of powerful authority in the best tradition of Freud.

#40: PIE TIME

Answer

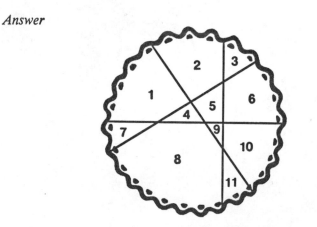

#41: PATTERNS OF THE MIND

Examples of responses
(1) Two Indian fakirs contemplating their navels (2) Two snakes in the throes of death-agony (3) A serpent with his shadow, chasing something (4) A man with bowed head kneeling in front of his dead pet snake (5) Chinese character (6) A bird seen from above (7) Someone pushing to get out of a bag (8) A screaming man reacting to a bird perched on a tree (9) Profile of a face with headdress (10) Pieces of discarded intestines (11) A man lying down, thinking (12) Two figures with heads lowered, lying down (13) A fetus (14) A person pouring water out of something (15) A person carrying a rock on his head (16) A woman in front of her vanity (17) Chinese scroll or Jewish script (18) A person, curled up, bouncing on a bed (19) Two dogs, one is watching a bone (20) Mountain range in the distance (21) Hunched-up cat

(1) A small boy with his fist up challenging someone to fight him (2) Skeleton of a dinosaur (3) An animal in the act of swallowing a prey too big for it to handle (4) A bird balancing a worm on its head (5) A bird flying through the clouds (6) A skeleton of an animal buried in white sand (7) A bird sitting on a branch (8) Genie coming out of a bottle (9) A half-bird, half-human figure (10) A very proud animal (11) Somebody twirling a lasso (12) Two heads with long necks (13) A rabbit running (14) An animal that has been shot, falling down (15) A bird sitting on a rock (16) A baby in white clothes (17) A seal and a duck (18) Big worm in the stomach (19) A belly dancer dancing and a dog jumping on the sidewalk.

#42: WHAT'S LOVE LIKE?

Examples
Love is a fire that burns and sparkles
In men as naturally as in charcoals.—SAMUEL BUTLER
Love's like the measles—all the worse when it comes late in life.—DOUGLAS JERROLD

Love, like the creeping vine, withers if it has nothing to embrace.—Nɪsuᴍɪ

Love, like cough, can't be hidden.—Aɴoɴʏᴍous

True love is like ghosts, which everybody talks about and few have seen.—Rᴏᴄʜᴇғoᴜᴄᴀᴜʟᴅ

Love is like the moon: when it does not increase, it decreases. —Sᴇǫᴜʀ

Love is like a child,
   That longs for everything that he can come by.
—Sʜᴀᴋᴇsᴘᴇᴀʀᴇ

Love, like a pirate, takes you by spreading false colors.
—Joʜɴ Vᴀɴʙʀᴜɢʜ

Love, like fortune, turns upon a heel, and is very much given to rising and falling.—Joʜɴ Vᴀɴʙʀᴜɢʜ

Love, like ambition, dies as 'tis enjoyed.—Tʜoᴍᴀs Yᴀʟᴅᴇɴ

Love is like linen, often chang'd the sweeter.
—Pʜɪɴᴇᴀs Fʟᴇᴛᴄʜᴇʀ

Love, like reputation, once fled, never returns more.
—Aᴘʜʀᴀ Bᴇʜɴ

#43: BOUNDARIES, SHAPES, AND SIZES

Answers

1.

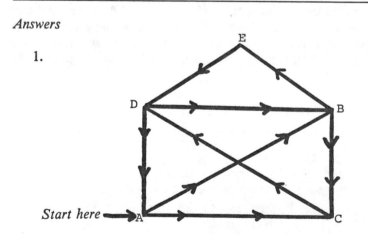

2.

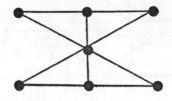

3.

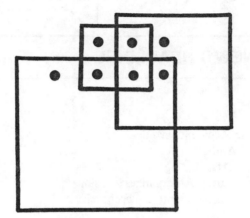

4.

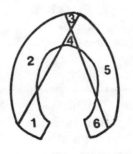

5.

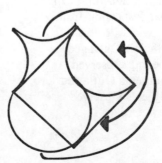

6.

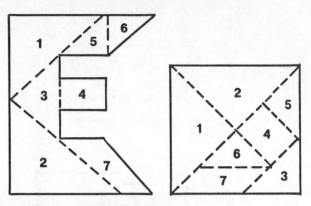

#44: NEWS HEADLINES

Examples

A

    Airplane Accident Avoided
    Alcohol Addiction Acute
    Africans Attack Angola
    Administration Antagonizes Alaska
    Automation Accelerates Absenteeism

E

    Entertainers Exchange Expletives
    English Explorer Expatriates
    Extensive Epidemic Erupts
    Extremist Escapes Execution
    European Exports Escalate

I

    Indonesia's Invasion Imminent
    Incumbent's Inaugural Inanities
    Inebriated Industrialist Indicted
    Important Invention Imminent
    International Inspection Insured

O

    Olympic Officials Outraged
    Opera's Opening Observed
    Occult Ornaments Outlawed
    Ominous Objects Observed
    Owner Obeys Order

U
    Urban Unemployed Unhappy
    Ukrainian Uprising Unsuccessful
    Urgent Ultimatum Undertaken
    University's Undergraduates Unappreciated
    Unscrupulous Undertaker Uncovered

#45: RADAR PALINDROME

Answer

The maximum number of ways anyone has been able to spell RADAR in this problem is 400.

#46: POLARITIES

Answers

1. Timid—Aggressive
2. Affinity—Aversion
3. Natural—Artificial
4. Scarce—Abundant
5. Relative—Absolute
6. Reject—Accept
7. Retard—Advance
8. Opponent—Associate
9. Unfinished—Accomplished
10. Increase—Abridge
11. Remote—Accessible
12. Discard—Agreement
13. Enlarge—Abbreviate
14. Consequent—Antecedent
15. Fail—Accomplish
16. Insufficient—Adequate
17. Deny—Agree
18. Unreal—Actual
19. Deliberate—Accidental
20. Expend—Amass
21. Rational—Absurd
22. Certainty—Ambiguity
23. Cool—Ardent
24. Real—Artificial
25. Dissimilar—Alike
26. Gradual—Abrupt

It is interesting to note that many researchers who have seriously studied the characteristics of creative persons have been struck by the many opposite, contradictory, or paradoxical coexisting qualities they possess. For example, they are at the same time confident yet somehow humble, detached yet intimately involved, relaxed yet attentive, discontented yet constructive, selfish yet disinterested, flexible yet persistent, spontaneous yet deliberate, accepting yet critical, and so on. One very intriguing and valuable definition of creativity also takes account of the presence of simultaneous antitheses. Thus, George M. Prince, president of Synectics, Inc., defines creativity as: "an arbitrary harmony, an expected astonishment, an habitual revelation, a familiar surprise, a generous selfishness, an unexpected certainty, a formable stubborness, a vital triviality, a disciplined freedom, an intoxicating steadiness, a repeated initiation, a difficult delight, a predictable gamble, an ephemeral solidity, a unifying difference, a demanding satisfier, a miraculous expectation, an accustomed amazement."

#47: ODD ONE OUT

Answers

1. Achievement	6. Concession	11. Psychiatrist
2. Admit	7. Talented	12. Game
3. Cherish	8. Exasperated	13. List
4. Resoluteness	9. Astrology	14. Impression
5. Idea	10. Faithful	

#48: HOW OB (LI)VIOUS II

Answers

1. He piled the earth in a mound until he reached the skylight.
2. She had been waiting inside a building.
3. Put the pants on backward.
4. They were facing each other.
5. Four inches. Since it is the record that turns, and not the stylus that travels around the record, the number of grooves is irrelevant to the problem. From the outer margin the stylus travels 4 inches toward the center of the disc—half the diameter, less half the inner blank plus the outer blank.

6. 3 of diamonds, 4 of diamonds, 4 of hearts.
7. Twelve.
8. $15. The horse cost $70 and the pig $15, a total of $85.
9. Socks, stockings, shoes, slippers, sandals, sneakers, snow-shoes, skis, skates, and so on.
10. Period, comma, colon, semicolon, interrogation mark, exclamation point, dash, hyphen, quotation marks, apostrophe, brackets, parentheses, braces, ellipses.

#49: WANT TO MAKE SOMETHING OF IT?

Examples

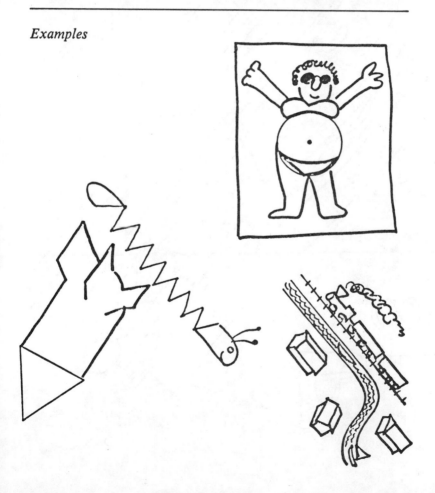

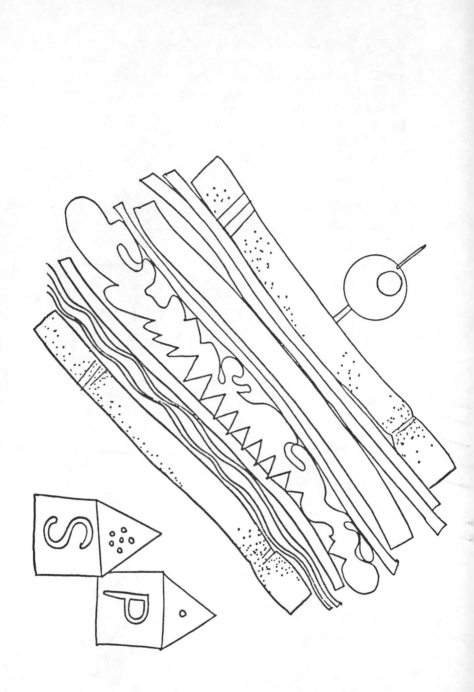

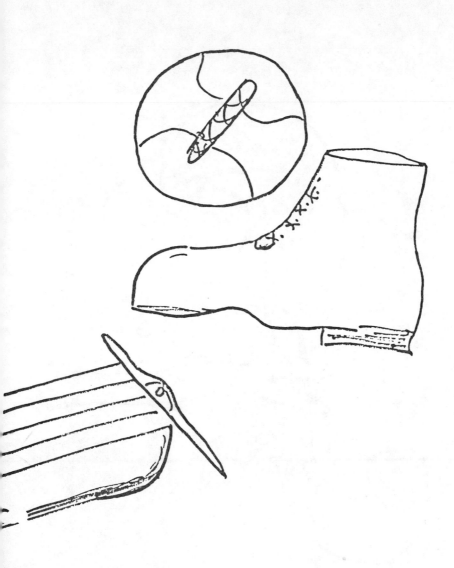

#50: BUILD A BRIDGE

Examples
1. Old *hat* shop
2. Fire *insurance* premium
3. Free *fall* guy
4. Fish *story* book
5. Expense *account* number
6. Iron *will power* block
7. Sleep *walk straight* line
8. Minute *hand book* maker
9. White *house dog tag* laundry
10. Brain *power play ball* game
11. Power *pack suitcase rack* brains
12. Black *paint brush aside* remark
13. Shell *game cock sure* thing
14. Nuclear *bomb bay window shopping* bag
15. Blank *check out last chance* upon
16. Body *English flag stop traffic* jam
17. Nose *ring bell hop over* time
18. Eagle *scout master hand downs beat* drums
19. Fuel *cell wall flower girl scout* master
20. Land *mine gold watch pocket veto* power
21. Foul *play around town house arrest burglar* alarm
22. Hair *shirt button collar bone dry run* scared

These associations are *examples* only. You may have found different and equally valid words of your own.

#51: EMPTY BOTTLE BINGE

Examples
Cut 1 inch from bottom and use as culture dish.
Use as saucer under plant.
Cut off 4 or 6 inches and use as planting pot.
Cut into bands and use as hoops for mobiles.
Cut into a continuous spiral for use as a mobile.

Use as a flexible container for mixing plaster of paris.
Cut into rings and use as molds for colored concrete discs for patio base.
Punch drain holes and use as a birdhouse.
Seal tight and use as floats for anchorage for small boats.
Tie two together as a swimming aid.
Use as base for a flower arrangement.
Add a few pebbles and use as a noise or rhythm instrument.
Fill with hot water and use as a foot warmer.
Cut and use as a yarn container-dispenser when knitting.
Cut eyes, nose, and mouth and use as a Halloween lantern.
Cut holes or diamond sl apes and use as patio light.
Float bottoms (cut to 1 ınch) with candles in ponds to attract bugs for fish food.
Cut off bottom and use for boat baler.
Cut off bottom and shape into a scoop for feed, sugar, and so on.
Punch holes, insert clothespins, color, and decorate as a piggy bank.

#52: DISCERNMENT

Examples

men	dent	diet	dirt	inset	cement
ten	dice	dime	meed	inter	indent
den	mine	mite	ides	medic	insect
cede	mire	need	denim	miter	tennis
cent	seed	nest	deter	dement	resent
cite	rite	cried	meter	decent	center
ice	tern	crime	merit	trine	censer
die	tide	deist	dinner	stern	insert
dim	miner	mince	desert	stein	intern
din	timer	midst	miser	direct	remind
tie	rent	mend	miter	entire	remise
dcem	rest	meet	trice	credit	endemic
deer	rice	dine	enter	cretin	metrics
mien	crest	dint	inert	rinse	centime
mere	creed	nice	disc	since	cistern

rim	time	nine	edit	niece	descent
met	trim	reed	emit	remit	discern
end	cider	rein	emir	reset	centner
ere	edict	ride	rind	incest	increment
mind	eider	rife	rise	recite	
side	mist	dire	send	reside	

#53: HORSING AROUND

The Solution

Step one

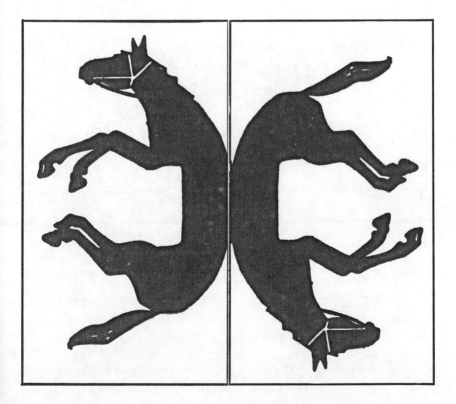

#54: EMPATHETIC SENSITIVITY

Examples

H. needs sympathy and understanding, but wife thinks only of herself.

W. wants to clear the air on occasion with a constructive fight, but husband is supersensitive to any implied or explicit criticism.

H. is a workaholic and wife feels cheated and neglected.

W. takes husband for granted and husband needs to be appreciated.

W. only wants to share problems, not pleasures or enjoyment.

H. runs to mother to tell about marital problems and wife resents this.

H. & W. have completely separate goals and interests.

W. wants to share her ideas, aspirations, and values, but husband is only interested in his ideas, aspirations, and values.

H. always wants to talk about the past, but wife wants to dream about the future.

H. wants to control wife but she insists on having her personal freedom.

#55: A LOVING CODE

If you had trouble translating the message, you can read it in a mirror if you place it on the edge of the dotted line. The message says: "Dearest Love."

#56: REVERSALS

Answer

To solve this problem you'll have to, in effect, accomplish two "reversals." You have to fold your arms and then grasp the diagonally opposite corners of the napkin. After you have unfolded your arms, the napkin will have a knot in it.

The reversal approach to problems has resolved many a "knotty" situation. For example, during World War II the enemy bombed U.S. planes before the pilots could get them out of the hangars and down the runways. Appalled by this calamity, the Air Force kept pondering ways to speed up the process of getting planes out of the hangars. No one came up with a satisfactory solution, until someone reversed the question to "How can we get the hangars away from the planes?" This new viewpoint brought a breakthrough solution: a diamond-shaped, two-section hangar, 172 feet long, that pulled apart at the widest point of the diamond. Mounted on rubber tires, the sections moved at 35 miles an hour, and when they moved, all the planes could take off at once.

#57: MAKING OPPORTUNITIES

Examples
The following are some examples provided by ten subscribers to *Creativity in Action* in different parts of the world.

Use rubbish to make collages or sculptures.
Collect antiques.
Invent musical/speaking dustbins (e.g., What do you think of it so far? Rubbish!).
Combine bird-watching with daily duties.
Organize dustmen's dances, garbage galas, or collectors' conventions.

Designate a National Dustbin Day.

Coordinate a dustman of the year competition or a "Get to know your dustman" campaign.

Wear spacemen outfits for fun.

Play dustbin games with kids.

Bestow dustmen's awards for gorgeous garbage.

Design a garbage barrel to suit your collection, i.e., size, shape, ease of carrying, wheels.

Design a household-garbage barrel to suit the particular needs of the community.

Keep a watch on the routing of the garbage truck, taking into account new houses and streets, to get the most economical routes.

Design a garbage uniform which is distinctive, protective, and adds a tone to the job.

Be cheerful to inject a happy thought to all householders.

Be prepared to help a householder who has a problem.

Keep watch on houses owned by old age pensioners.

Collect specific types of garbage for recycling.

Act as a tester for clothing in hardwearing conditions.

Sort the garbage and extract salable and repairable items. Incidentally, OXFAM does just this.

Be a "Peeping Tom" (or possibly more for bored housewives!).

Leave a clear, tidy area around the garbage area, and be proud to do so. Have a competition for the tidiest area.

Find out the shortest way through town.

Find out the best places to stop, and mark them.

Find the best ways to handle barrels and to lift and empty them.

Start a garbage market for usable items.

Find ways to pick up the garbage automatically—for example a vacuum sucker.

Develop a kind of fermentation tank for people to make humus for their gardens.

Combine garbage collecting and road cleaning.

Devise an additional service: for example, feed pets while people are on holiday.

Your own job is susceptible to the same processes and possibilities. Ask yourself the same question we asked about the garbage collector's job. Take some time out and see how many opportunities and new advantages you might think up for your own situation. Set yourself a target of 50 ideas. When you reach 50, see if you can get at least 25 more, even if you have to put the project aside for a few hours or a day. And remember—suspend your critical faculties and judgment while you are coming up with those ideas. The "kooky" ideas will eventually fall by the wayside, but they might be extremely useful in triggering some of the best ideas listed. That is where their value lies.

Finding new opportunities and new advantages for yourself often requires that you get yourself into motion when you're at the top or bottom dead-center position, seemingly unable to move.

I hope the preceding examples will give you the impetus for getting motion started from that dead-center position. It is well worth trying!

#58: WACKY WORDIES

Answers

1a Just between you and me
1b Hitting below the belt
1c Head over heels in love
1d Shrinking violets
1e Bermuda Triangle
1f A mixed bag
2a Cry over spilt milk
2b Lying in wait
2c Unfinished Symphony
2d Pineapple upside-down cake
2e You're under arrest
2f Split-second timing
3a Nothing on TV
3b Fly-by-night
3c Raise a big stink
3d Add insult to injury
3e Railroad crossing
3f A person after my own heart
4a At the point of no return
4b The inside dope
4c Long underwear
4d Ostrich with its head on the ground
4e Lucky break
4f Corner the market
5a World without end
5b Way behind the times
5c Word to the wise
5d Search high and low
5e Go off half-cocked
5f No two ways about it
6a Hole-in-one
6b Down-to-earth
6c Three-ring circus
6d One at a time
6e Better late than never
6f Get a word in edgewise
7a Let bygones be bygones
7b An outside chance
7c Three degrees below zero
7d A terrible spell of weather
7e World Series

#59: AS QUICK AS A WINK

Examples

As quick as . . . an arrow, a flash, a flame, hell can scorch a
feather, a stab, a storm, a darted beam of light, the blink of an eye,
a wink, a dart, a torrent's run, an unruly deluge, a dog will lick a
dish, the streaming rain, an eagle flies through the air, fall days
slide toward winter, flying clouds, a sun's ray, a lover's dream, a
star falls through the night, a whirlwind, a tornado, a missile tear-
ing up the sky, and so on.

Meaning slow

Examples

As quick as . . . a plumber going for his tools, cold molasses, a
worm, a snail, a broken-winded mare, a man in doubt, a passing
cloud when there is no wind, the completion of a boring task, a
teenager's telephone conversation, eternity, a policeman writing out
a ticket, a pregnant cow moving on ice, a commercial on TV, good
fortune coming, a burning match, a Sunday afternoon's passing.

One eminently effective technique to increase creativity is
called Synectics, developed by William J. J. Gordon. It essentially
involves approaching a problem through the deliberate evocation of
metaphors, similes, and analogies. For example, one of the problems Gordon's group tackled was the invention of a new kind of roof
that would be white in summer (reflecting heat) and black in winter
(absorbing heat). The initial metaphoric associations of the group
included discussion about things in nature that change color such as
weasels, chameleons, and flounders. One group member pointed out
that the flounder changes color by releasing pigment from lower
layers of skin to higher ones. This observation triggered a sudden

flash of insight in another member of the group: build the roof out of black material with tiny white balls in it which will expand when the roof gets hot, rise, and turn the roof white. The Synectics method encourages people to become aware of metaphors, similes, and images from their subconscious with unimpeded directness.

#60: VARIETIES OF CREATIVITY

The following are the characteristics that are usually checked by the different types. Remember that there are no *pure* classifications and your self-perceptions may span several different categories, adding individuality and variety to your creative style.

Extraverted Thinking	*Introverted Thinking*
Dominant	Analytical
Practical	Independent
Bold	Quiet
Disciplined	Disciplined
Objective	Curious
Analytical	Adaptable
Conscientious	Clear thinking
Logical	Intellectual
Decisive	Organized
Energetic	Logical
Confident	Persistent
Responsible	Efficient
Determined	Thoughtful

Extraverted Intuitive	*Introverted Intuitive*
Innovative	Creative
Enthusiastic	Persevering
Imaginative	Ingenious
Confident	Understanding
Persistent	Soft-spoken
Involved	Reserved
Stimulating	Intelligent
Perceptive	Sincere
Persuasive	Observant
Forward-looking	Determined

Mature	Patient
Serious	Persistent
Energetic	Frank

Extraverted Sensing	*Introverted Sensing*
Realistic	Dependable
Factual	Stable
Persuasive	Thorough
Openminded	Factual
Easygoing	Systematic
Tolerant	Painstaking
Efficient	Persevering
Quick	Reliable
Calm	Practical
Considerate	Objective
Tactful	Serious-minded
Diplomatic	Effective
Friendly	Conservative

Extraverted Feeling	*Introverted Feeling*
Friendly	Modest
Tactful	Cooperative
Warm	Sincere
Cooperative	Loyal
Enthusiastic	Understanding
Cheerful	Tolerant
Agreeable	Sensitive
Understanding	Sympathetic
Considerate	Committed
Loyal	Independent
Idealistic	Controlled
Sympathetic	Soft-spoken
Gracious	Patient

The descriptions that follow analyze the eight basic types of creative personalities previously mentioned. Each type's creative style is described.

Extraverted-Thinking Type—"But the facts are . . ."

The extraverted-thinking type likes to take charge of things and run the whole show.

A disciplined thinker, this person respects objectivity, well-thought-out plans, and orderly procedures. Being strongly analytical and objectively critical, he or she is unlikely to be creative about, or persuaded by, anything but clear reasoning and logic. According to him, everyone's focus should be governed strictly by logic, and he is his own stern taskmaster in this respect. He likes innovation that involves facts, figures, and concrete matters.

He enjoys manipulating the real world, and is unstinting in his efforts to act upon and implement his ideas. He likes to make decisions, is good at organizing plans and projects, and enjoys interplay with others. If his creative plans are carried out half-heartedly, he is capable of losing his temper. He tends to demand recognition of his performance by others, and believes that his approach to innovation and decision making is the only right one. Being strongwilled, he can intimidate people with ease and without feelings of guilt.

Introverted-Thinking Type—"I'll have to give it some further thought."

The introverted-thinking person prefers to analyze rather than control. He or she is good at creatively organizing ideas and facts, rather than people and situations. When absorbed in analysis or creative problem-solving, he remains markedly independent of external circumstances. He shows great perseverance and can easily work uninterruptedly on one novel idea for a long time, frequently to the exclusion of almost everything else.

Outwardly quiet, reserved, and sometimes withdrawn, he can be detachedly curious about what is going on, and can be adaptable as long as his inner ruling principles are not violated. Although confident in the realm of ideas, this person requires time to arrive at decisions requiring action and implementation. He is ideally suited to working out the difficulties underlying a complex problem. Others can then do the implementing.

His or her major shortcoming is difficulty in communicating. The introverted-thinking type can state his creative ideas and solutions clearly and exactly, but keeps them so exact, abstract, and complicated that others frequently find it difficult to follow him.

Extraverted-Intuitive Type—"I have a hunch."

The extraverted-intuitive man or woman is the ebulliently enthusiastic innovator. Possessing a great deal of imagination, he or she constantly perceives new possibilities or new ways of doing things. This person is happiest dreaming up and initiating new ideas, and, by getting others involved, usually carries them out.

He is confident of the worth of his ideas, tireless in problem solving, and shows great ingenuity in tackling the difficulties or snags encountered. Having patience and stick-to-itiveness with complicated situations, this person can almost always be relied upon to discover creative solutions that work. He gets so involved in ideas that he thinks of little else.

Another of his positive attributes is the ability to animate, stimulate, and persuade others to accept his ideas. His perceptive and empathetic understanding of people enables him to win ready support.

His biggest problem is his aversion to uninspired routine, and he can hardly force himself to attend to humdrum details or projects alien to his major interests. Even his pet projects begin to pall and lose their challenge with time. What will happen next is more significant to him than what is happening in the here-and-now. As a result, he is happiest and most productive with a variety of creative challenges. Other individuals can then do the implementing once the major problems are solved.

Introverted-Intuitive Type—"Silence—genius at work."

This person is conventionally recognized as the true creator. He or she completely trusts intuitive insights. Complex and ambiguous problems stimulate him, and he sees many possibilities in situations that appear to others as "closed."

He tends to drive his associates as intensely as his own ideas drive him, and he backs up his creative insights with determination. He likes to have his ideas worked out, applied and accepted, and will spend any amount of time and effort to achieve this goal.

His Achilles' heel is his singleminded concentration and abhorrence of compromise. At times he seems so blinded by the value of his ideas and plans that he fails to see the conditions, circumstances, or other counterforces that should be taken into account.

This person is effective in situations where boldly ingenious creativity is needed. Although his boldness may be of great value, reality-check is mandatory.

He creates in bursts of energy powered by excitement and enthusiasm, and feels smothered in routine full of small details. Where he may be lacking most is in judgment. He can not comfortably listen to outside judgment or criticism of his ideas and insights, and is, at times, in danger of ignoring the real world. Not always having the power to shape his ideas into effective action, he may appear to others as an impractical genius or crank, or simply a dreamer who indulges in fruitless fantasy.

He is little involved with others and needs minimal companionship.

Extraverted-Sensing Type—"The right tool for the right job."

This person is an adaptable realist who is keenly attuned to the concrete, the actual, and the factual. He always knows what the facts are because he notices, absorbs, and remembers more of them than anyone else around. There is a sort of effortless economy in the way he tackles concrete situations. Coupled with the ability to see and consider the needs of the moment is his resourcefulness in implementing plans and projects without delay.

Being a perceptive person, the extraverted-sensing type searches for the satisfying creative solution, instead of trying to impose any "should" or "ought" of his own; and his associates usually accept the unique compromises he arrives at. He tends to be openminded, easygoing, unprejudiced, and tolerant of almost everyone. He knows how to manage conflict and is good at easing a tense situation or pulling warring factions together to bring a new creative idea into function.

Introverted-Sensing Type—"The real meaning is not what it seems."

This person is very dependable. Like his extraverted-sensing counterpart, he also handles facts with ease, and can absorb, remember, and use a tremendous number of them. Everything for him has to be clearly stated and put on a factual basis before he attacks the issue.

He reacts to facts and problems in an individualistic way, but what he actually does about them is usually sound and valid. This is because he senses the deeper aspect of things. In his creative problem-solving he is thorough, painstaking, and systematic. He is patient with detail and routine and his persevering attitude has a stabilizing effect on others around him.

This person does not leap impulsively into projects, but once involved, it is difficult to distract, discourage, or stop him; and he is unstinting in the effort and time he expends. Unless circumstances convince him that he is on a wrong track, he will persist.

His practical judgment, memory for detail, and conservative bent make him consistent and reliable. He can always be counted on to cite cases to support his ideas. Responsibilities of maintenance and implementation are ideally suited for him.

His shortcoming is that he cannot readily empathize with needs that diverge radically from what he perceives are the needs of a situation, and he is apt to dismiss them out of hand. In his interpersonal relationships this person tends to be impersonal and rather passive. He accepts others as long as they don't try to interfere with what he is producing.

Extraverted-Feeling Type—"The more the merrier."

This person radiates good fellowship and is sensitive to emotional atmosphere. In relationships with others, he or she tends to be friendly, tactful, and sympathetic. Since his sense of security and well-being derives from the warmth of others, he can become quite upset by any display of indifference. Other people constitute the source for his creative inspirations.

The obvious forte of this type of person is in situations that deal with people, and he does his best creative thinking when talking with others. He is good at greeting people and often enjoys long telephone conversations, during which he gets many of his ideas. For him to be brief and businesslike requires special effort.

Since this person has to be constantly involved and interacting with others to be inspired, he tends to be impatient with long, slow situations or complicated procedures, especially when these require solitary absorption. His other shortcoming is tending to jump to conclusions and acting upon assumptions which may be wide of the mark.

He is drawn to those having similar creative traits and interests, and can be insensitive or blind to conflict and potentially explosive interpersonal situations, because of his strong desire to ignore unpleasant feelings and disharmony.

Introverted Feeling Type—"Still waters run deep."

This person has as much wealth of feeling as the feeling extravert, but he or she focuses more deeply on fewer things and has greater inner intensity. He, like the feeling extravert, puts duty and obligations first, but is more strongly guided by inner-directed values in the search for creative ideas and solutions.

He can be understanding, tolerant, and sensitive to other people's feelings as long as his deepest values and convictions are not challenged or threatened. He prefers to be left alone when problem solving, and has little need to impress, change, or persuade others.

He creates best when working at something he believes in, and his feelings add extra spark to his efforts. There has to be a personally meaningful purpose behind his effort—he has to work on things that matter.

The main problem of this person is that he tends to be overly sensitive and vulnerable to criticism and frequently suffers from a sense of inadequacy, even though he may be just as creative as the other types.

He exhibits practiced control of feelings, and his true motives generally remain concealed and secret. He is able to suppress negative feelings and judgments in an attempt to keep unpleasant situations at a distance.

#61: FROM A TO Z

Examples

Accountant   Advertising copy writer*   Architect*

Artist*
Athletic coach*
Attorney
Auditor†
Auto mechanic
Ballet dancer*
Banker†
Biologist*
Bookkeeper†
Botanist
Buyer*
Carpenter*
Cashier†
Chauffeur†
Chef*
Chemist*
Civil engineer*
Clerk†
Collector†
Compensation manager
Composer*
Controller†
Counselor*
Data Processor*
Dean of College
Dentist†
Designer*
Dietitian
Dishwasher†
Draftsperson*
Driver†
Economist*
Editor*
EDP analyst*
Educator*
Electrician†
Employment manager*
Engineer*
Entertainer*
Executive
Exporter
Farmer
Fashion model*
Field service technician
File clerk
Financial analyst
Fitness instructor
Florist*
Forrester
Funeral director†
Gal/guy Friday

Gardener
Geologist*
Graphic artist*
Guard†
Hairstylist*
Handyman*
Historian
Home health nurse
Hostess/host
Hotel manager*
Importer
Industrial engineer*
Insurance underwriter†
Investment broker*
Jazz pianist*
Jet set loafer
Jeweler*
Jockey
Journalist*
Judge
Justice of the peace
Kangaroo trainer
Kapellmeister*
Kennel keeper
Keypunch operator†
Kindergarten teacher
Kitchen maid
Laboratory technician
Lawyer
Legal secretary
Librarian
Machinist
Mailroom clerk†
Management consultant*
Manager*
Market researcher*
Messenger†
Minister
Model*
Musician*
Narcotics pusher
Navigator
Necrologist
Negotiator
Neurologist
Nurse*
Occupational therapist*
Office Manager
Offset pressman†
Optician
Optometrist

Painter*
Paper cutter†
Payroll clerk†
Personnel manager
Pharmacist
Photographer*
Physical therapist
Physician†
Pilot
Placement counselor*
Plant manager*
Plasterer
Plumber
Poet*
Politician†
Priest
Printer
Programmer*
Promoter*
Proofreader†
Psychiatrist
Psychologist*
Public Relations Manager*
Publisher*
Purchasing agent
Quadrille instructor
Quality Control Manager
Quantitative analyst
Quarterback
Quartermaster
Rabbi
Radiologist
Real Estate Salesperson
Receptionist†
Reporter*
Researcher*
Research scientist*
Respiratory therapist
Restaurant manager
Retail manager
Rodeo performer
Salesperson*
Scientist*
Sculptor*
Secretary
Statistician
Superintendent
Supervisor
Systems analyst*
Tailor
Tax collector

Taxicab driver†	Ventriloquist*	Xerox repairman†
Teacher*	Veterinarian	X-ray technician
Technician	Vice squad officer	Xylographer
Telephone operator†	Violinist*	Xylophonist*
Travel agent	Vocational counselor*	Yachts-man
Tree surgeon	Vydec operator	Yellow journalist
TV repairman	Waiter	Yeoman
Typist	Wall Street analyst*	Yodeler
Undertaker†	Warehouse manager	Yogi
Upholsterer	Watchmaker	Youth counselor*
Vagabond	Well driller†	Zincographer
Valet	Wine taster	Zither player*
Vanity press publisher	Woodworker	Zoo director
Varsity coach*	Word processor	Zookeeper
Vendor	Writer*	Zoologist*

Preliminary research data from the Institute of Personality Research Assessment of the University of California, Berkeley, indicate that persons in occupations marked with an asterisk are generally more creative than are those indicated with a dagger. The rest can fall into either category.

Notable exceptions, of course, exist in all careers and occupations. A housewife, an electrician, or a retail manager can be more creative than a painter, a designer, or a scientist. But chances are strong that if your "Like" list included more of the occupations regarded as *creative*, and your "Dislike" list contained those considered *less creative*, that you have a creative predisposition.

#62: KILLER PHRASES

Part I
Examples
    We've never done it that way before.
    We haven't the manpower.
    It's not in the budget.
    All right in theory but can you put it into practice?
    Too academic.
    What will the customers think.
    Somebody would have suggested it before if it were any good.
    Too modern.

Too old-fashioned.
Let's discuss it some other time.
You don't understand our problem.
We're too small for that.
We're too big for that.
We have too many projects now.
Let's make a market research test first.
What bubblehead thought that up?
Let's form a committee.
Let's think it over for a while and watch developments.
That's not our problem.
Production won't accept it.
They'll think we're long-haired.
Engineering can't do it.
Won't work in my territory.
Customers won't stand for it.
You'll never sell that to management.
Don't move too fast.
The union will scream.
Here we go again.
No adolescent is going to tell *me* how to run my business!

Part II
Examples

This may not be applicable, but . . .
While we have only made a few preliminary tests . . .
This approach is screwy, but . . .
I don't know if the money can be appropriated, but . . .
It might be a dead end, but . . .
Do you suppose it would be possible to . . .
It may take a long time, but . . .
It may sound harebrained, but . . .
I don't know just what you want, but . . .
You probably have ideas about this too, but . . .
You aren't going to like this, but . . .
This is contrary to policy, but . . .
This may not be the right time, but . . .
This idea seems useless, but . . .
You can probably do this better, but . . .

If I were younger and had my health . . .
I suppose our competitors have already tried this, but . . .
I'm not too familiar with this, but . . .
This may be too expensive, but . . .
I don't know what is in the literature on this, but . . .
This is not exactly on this subject, but . . .
I haven't thought this one through, but . . .
You'll probably laugh, but . . .
My opinions are not worth much, but . . .
I'm no genius, but . . .
I don't get enthused over this idea myself, but . . .
It may not be important, but . . .
This will need further study, but . . .
If you'll take the suggestion of a novice . . .
Now here's a sketchy idea of what I have in mind, for you to
kick holes in . . .

#63: CREATIVE LISTENING

Examples

She never looks at me while I'm talking. It's hard to tell for
sure if she's even listening.

He constantly fidgets with his glasses, a pencil, a letter opener,
or something—looking at and examining the object rather than listening to me.

She always gets me off the subject with her questions and comments.

He always tries to anticipate what I'm going to say next, and
jumps ahead to tell me my next point.

She rephrases what I say in such a way that she puts words into
my mouth.

Occasionally he asks a question about what I have just said,
which shows he just was not listening. For example, after I finish
telling him about a problem, he might ask, "Let's see, what was the
problem you wanted to talk to me about?"

When I talk to him he doesn't stop what he's doing to give me
his complete attention.

She doesn't give me a chance to talk. I state a problem but never do get a chance to tell about it.

She often gives me the feeling that I'm wasting my time.

He argues with almost everything I say—often even before I have had a chance to state my case.

He sits there picking his nails, or cleaning them, or cleaning his glasses, or fiddling with a cigarette, and I know he can't do that and listen attentively.

She acts as if she's just waiting for me to get through talking in order to interject something of her own.

When I have a good idea, he always says, "Yeah, I've been thinking about that too."

He stares at me as if trying to outstare me.

He overdoes trying to show me he is following what I am saying—too many nods of the head, yeahs, and uh-huh's.

She tries to insert humorous remarks when I am trying to be serious.

She frequently sneaks looks at her watch or the clock while I am talking.

He often acts as if I am keeping him from doing something "important."

He asks questions that demand agreement. For example, he makes a statement and then says, "Don't you think so?" or "Don't you agree?"

His expression never changes; he never smiles. His grim countenance makes one apprehensive to talk.

Guidelines to Creative Listening

The following guidelines are presented to help you improve your listening awareness and efficiency.

Increase Your Listening Span. Deliberately try to inhibit your temptation to interrupt. Make sure the speaker has had the opportunity to make his or her point before you speak.

Take Time to Listen. If you put obvious limitations on your listening time, the speaker is apt to feel rushed. Initial statements are frequently only a vague approximation of what a person means. In order for the speaker to open up and crystallize his meaning, you must convey the feeling that he has the time to talk freely. Don't rationalize that you're too busy to listen.

Give Full Attention. Occasional nodding or interjected comments give the impression that you find the speaker interesting. If he pauses briefly, don't rush in to fill the silence, but wait for him to organize his thoughts and to express them. Once he is talking freely, let him speak until you're sure he has completed his statement. Then you can pose a question that encourages elaboration of certain points that were unclear or incomplete.

Restate the Message. When you are sure the speaker has finished, restate the main points in your own words and ask if he concurs with your meaning. This assures that any misunderstanding is kept at a minimum.

Avoid Hasty Evaluation. One of the major barriers to effective interpersonal communication is the tendency to judge, evaluate, approve, or disapprove too hastily the statement of the other person. To achieve real creative communication, you must inhibit this evaluative tendency and listen with understanding.

Don't Overreact to Delivery. "What a slow speaker!" "What a dull monotone voice she has!" "Who would want to listen to this drone!" Many of us have used such thoughts to tune a speaker out. A good listener is not concerned about the speaker's mannerisms or delivery. Instead, his attitude is: "What's in his message that I need to know?" "What can he add to my knowledge and experience?"

Don't Overreact to Content. Poor listening can also be attributed to getting overly excited or stimulated by what the speaker says, especially if he or she challenges one of the listener's convictions, pet peeves, or prejudices. From that moment on, emotional filters start operating and the listener is busy devising arguments to defend or bolster his convictions and negate those of the speaker. Any remaining remarks go largely unheard. A good listener suppresses excitement and suspends evaluation until all the evidence is in and tested.

Listen Between the Lines. Don't only listen to what is said, but try to understand the attitudes, needs, and motives that lie behind the words. Also, remember that the speaker does not always put his or her entire message into words. The changing tones and volume of the voice may have meaning; so may the facial expressions, gestures, and the movements of the body. Being alert to nonverbal cues increases your total comprehension of the speaker's message.

Listen for Ideas, Not Facts. The importance of names, dates, and places has been drilled into us since childhood. Hence, when we listen, we tend to focus on these facts rather than on underlying ideas. A good listener weighs and compares each fact to see what key idea binds them together.

#64: DELEGATION

Examples

She thinks it's easier to do the job herself rather than spend time explaining the work to a subordinate.

The meticulous planning that delegation requires—establishing priorities, setting objectives, formulating methods of approach, assigning individual tasks, and projecting the timespan required for completion—is not easy or worth the trouble.

He fears that a subordinate's judgment is faulty or that he will not follow through on his ideas.

He has been recently promoted, and feels insecure in his job and in his relationship with his superiors, peers, and subordinates. As a result, he regresses to the familiar security of routine work prior to promotion.

She feels overwhelmed and confused by her duties and responsibilities and cannot explain the work to subordinates.

He has a temperamental aversion to risk-taking, and feels that even with clear instructions, proper controls, and trained subordinates, something will go wrong.

She equates action with productivity and is afraid that delegation might leave her with nothing to do.

She feels it is a sign of weakness to need subordinates' help to keep up with the workload.

He fears that he might appear lazy.

She imitates her boss, whose style of leadership did not include delegating.

He feels that he has to justify his status and salary by overworking.

#65: FUTURE HEADLINES

Examples
   World Attains Zero Population Growth
   Weather Forecasting Now Reliable
   All Forms of Cancer Defeated
   Average Work Week Now Twenty Hours
   Forced Retirement Abolished
   Inaugurating Weekly Flights to the Moon
   Breakthrough in Ocean Farming Techniques
   Immunization Against All Viral Infections
   Life-long Learning Curriculums Established
   Full Control of Multi-National Corporations
   Tedium at Work Eliminated
   Creative Leisure Programs For Everyone
   Violence on Television Eliminated
   Effective Marriage Enrichment Programs
   Average Work Week Reduced to 22 Hours
   Sexual Equality Now a Reality
   Elimination of Planned Obsolescence
   Phone Calls Now Five Cents
   Organized Crime Eliminated
   Drug Problem Licked
   Pet Population Reduced
   Diabetes Now Curable
   All Peoples' Survival Needs Met
   Universal Meta-Language Adopted
   No More Hangovers
   All Waste Is Now Recycled
   Weather Control a Reality
   Use of Solar Energy Available to All
   90% of Illiteracy Eliminated
   New City in Atlantic Ocean Thriving

#66: STORY TIME

Examples
Dream, letter, day, castle, beach, surprise

I had a *dream* that finally my red-*letter-day* had arrived: my uncle had left me his huge *castle* overlooking a beautiful *beach* in Normandy. When I awoke, to my great *surprise* there was a telegram confirming that all this had actually happened.

Sea, woman, face, castle, boat, failure

Mrs. North, a middle-aged *woman* with three children, decided to leave her husband and go to *sea*. She purchased an old fishing *boat*, completed all the necessary repairs, and set off in search of her fortune. On the third day of her voyage she encountered a thick fog, and, as she moved slowly through it, she noticed a flashing light in the distance which lighted up the rocks nearby, giving them the appearance of a sea captain's *face*. She dropped anchor and rowed ashore to investigate. Above the light was a *castle* with one candle burning dimly in a lower window. Slowly, tremulously, she approached the window and inside saw a dejected old man sitting in a chair. He looked like her husband, only about 30 years older, and he was nearing the end of his life, feeling like a miserable *failure*. Mrs. North returned to her boat and sailed back to her family.

Sea, night, letter, marry, house, fate

The *sea* was churning in and out like two lovers together in the *night*. A bottle hit the side of my pitching dory. I picked it up, saw a white piece of paper inside, uncorked the bottle, and pulled out what looked like a short *letter*. "Dearest, dearest Charlie"—my God, my name!—"I beg, I beg you to *marry* me before darkness, Pristine." I had never even heard of a name like Pristine. What *house*, if any on the shore had this bottle come from? Would I, at last, by *fate*, after 41 years have a woman who wanted me?

Ghost, birthday, house, night, start, song

There was a friendly *ghost* who visited me on my *birthday*. He arrived at my *house* late at *night* and couldn't wait to *start* singing a *song* he had just composed to celebrate this great occasion.

Accident, money, luck, doctor, police, car

I once had a bad *accident* that cost me a lot of *money*. I felt I was really down on my *luck*. When I got the bill from the *doctor*, I couldn't pay him and one day he arrived at my home in a *police car* announcing that he would put me under citizen's arrest. I laughed at him. This angered him so much that he had a heart attack and died.

#67: WHAT IF . . .

Examples
What would happen if . . .
you were the only person in the world?
no one ever had to work?
murder were declared legal?
nothing ever changed?
everyone had to work 20 hours a day?
all money were destroyed?
everyone spoke without thinking?
all your friends turned into enemies?
all our wishes were satisfied?
there were no armies?
all babies were grown in testtubes?
marriage were prohibited?
you felt like a different person every other day?
all sports were outlawed?
no one ever felt guilty or ashamed?
everyone loved his brother as himself?
everyone failed at everything he or she ever tried?
children never grew up?
parents were never allowed to see their children?
one person had all the money in the world?
everyone felt tired all the time?
all religions were abolished?
everyone were drunk all the time?
everyone did everything he would like to do?
people couldn't marry until they were 50?
all the books were destroyed?
we were always feeling very emotional?
everyone did exactly what he or she felt like?

#68: FOLLOW YOUR HUNCHES

As a "mental shortcut," intuition has been responsible for the dramatic success stories of many prominent inventors and businessmen. One classic case is that of Dr. Edwin H. Land, president of Polaroid Corporation and inventor of the Polaroid camera. His original invention met with stiff resistance from his associates. Extensive market research indicated that there would be little or no demand for the camera; it would be too expensive to be sold as a toy and not up to the standards demanded of a fine camera. Fortunately, Dr. Land's intuition prevailed and he became the central figure in one of the all-time success stories in business.

Another prominent industrialist who sustained a hunch with great courage is George I. Long, then president of Ampex Corporation. Right after the war, when the television boom started, Long "guessed" that a product permitting the transcriptions of TV programs for distribution and rebroadcast would tap a huge potential market. Several other firms had considered the idea and had conducted preliminary research. But they all felt that the technical difficulties were too great and were dubious about the potential market value of the product. Ampex at that time considered itself too small to tackle the problem, but so strong was George Long's hunch about the success of such a product that the company risked the costly development project anyway. The decision was fortunate—the hunch paid off. The result was videotape, which established Ampex as a leader in the industry.

What is Intuition? Although any single definition of intuitive thinking is almost certain to be incomprehensible, the process can be defined "operationally." It is a form of reasoning in which the weighing and balancing of evidence is carried out unconsciously.

Intuitive versus Analytical Modes. Further clarification can be obtained by comparing intuitive thinking to the analytical mode of thinking. Dr. Jerome S. Bruner compares the two this way: "Analytic thinking characteristically proceeds a step at a time. Steps are explicit and usually can be adequately reported by the thinker to another individual. Such thinking proceeds with relatively full awareness of the information and operations involved. . . .

"Intuitive thinking usually does not advance in careful, well-

175

defined steps. Indeed, it tends to involve maneuvers based seemingly on an implicit perception of the total problem. The thinker arrives at an answer, which may be right or wrong, with little if any awareness of the process by which he reached it. He rarely can provide an adequate account of how he obtained his answer, and may be unaware of just what aspects of the problem situation he was responding to."

Professor George Turin of the University of California, Berkeley, states that the following elements are involved in an "intuitive approach" to problem solving:

•The ability to know how to attack a problem without quite being sure *how* you know

•The ability to relate a problem in one field to seemingly different problems in other fields

•The ability to recognize what is peripheral and what is central, without having understood the problem fully

•The ability to know in advance the general nature of the solution

•The ability to recognize when a solution *must* be right, first because "it feels right"

Intuition and Creativity. Is there any experimental evidence that a high correlation exists between intuitive ability and creativity? In an extensive study, Dr. Donald W. MacKinnon and his associates at the University of California tested hundreds of creative and noncreative subjects in a number of fields. One of the tests used was the Myers-Briggs Type Indicator, which distinguishes between two cognitive orientations—sense perception and intuitive perception. The person who favors sense perception is "inclined to focus upon his immediate sensory experience." He or she concentrates on the sensory attributes of the experience and centers the attention on existing facts as they are given. In contrast, the intuitive-perceptive person "immediately and instinctively perceives the deeper meanings and possibilities inherent in situations and ideas which he experiences." He is "ever alert to links and bridges between what is present and that which is not yet thought of." He focuses habitually upon what may be, rather than upon what is.

On this test, over 90 per cent of the creative subjects showed a marked preference for intuition. In the case of the less creative or noncreative individuals, the percentage preference for intuition was considerably lower. Dr. MacKinnon concludes: "It is not that this finding is surprising. One would not expect creative persons to be stimulus-and-object bound, but instead, ever alert to the as-yet-not realized. It is rather the *magnitude* of the preference for intuitive perception that is so striking among highly creative persons."

When Are Hunches Valid? Hunches can be validated only when acted upon and proven right or wrong. There are, however, some subjective clues used by people who believe in the intuitive hunch. They know, for example, that one characteristic of a valid hunch is the adherence to a keen sense of value. The hunch arrives brimming with positive feeling and a sense of certainty.

The person is sure, at the moment the hunch occurs, that he has grasped the core of the problem and has found the best alternative for solution. Doubt and uncertainty about the validity of the solution may occur later. But an individual who trusts his intuitive judgment seldom abandons it because of later doubts.

Sense of Compulsion. An intuitive hunch is often accompanied by a sense of immediacy which recurrently invades a person's consciousness. When engaged in some other activity, he often becomes distracted. He feels compelled to return to the implementation of the intuitive hunch, even though the time or occasion for considering it is not propitious. Thus, the intuitive hunch sometimes has the earmarks of compulsion. And it is usually wise to heed this compulsion.

#69: EVALUATING IDEAS

It is difficult if not impossible to devise a criteria checklist that would meet the requirements of all ideas, individuals, or situations with fidelity. You can use the following examples to add to or modify the list you come up with.

Evaluation Checklist Developed by Princeton Creative Research

1. Have you considered all the advantages or benefits of the idea? Is there a real need for it?

2. Have you pinpointed the exact problems or difficulty your idea is expected to solve?

3. Is your idea an original, new concept, or is it a new combination of known elements, a new adaptation?

4. What immediate or short-range gains or results can be anticipated? Are the projected returns adequate? Are the risk factors acceptable?

5. What long-range benefits can be anticipated? Will they support the company's objectives?

6. Have you checked the operational soundness of the idea? Can it be made by the company? Are the company's engineering, production, sales, and distribution facilities adequate for implementation?

7. Have you checked the idea for any faults or limitations?

8. Are there any problems the idea might create? What are the changes involved?

9. Have you considered the economic factors of its implementation—what talent, time for development, investment, marketing costs does it entail? What personnel will be involved? Who else is needed to perform the job? Which other divisions or departments will be affected?

10. How simple or complex will its execution or implementation be?

11. How well does it fit into the current operation of the organization?

12. Could you work out several variations of the idea, to afford those who will judge it a freedom of choice? Could you offer alternate ideas?

13. Does it have a natural sales appeal? How ready is the market for it? Can customers afford it? Will customers buy it? Is timing a factor?

14. What, if anything, is competition doing in this area? Can your company be competitive?

15. Have you considered the possible user resistances or difficulties?

16. Does your idea fill a real need or does the need have to be created through promotional and advertising efforts?

17. Is it compatible with other procedures or products of the company and its overall objectives?

18. Is it a right idea, or a right product area, for the organization?

19. Are there any specific circumstances in your organization that might make the acceptance of the idea difficult?

20. How soon could it be put into operation?

Questions for results. Here is a device which can be useful in evaluating ideas concerning almost any type of organizational problem:

If a company contemplated the introduction of a new product or process, the key factors upon which the evaluative criteria should be erected would be found in the analysis of the potential market and the product or process itself.

If the problem involves management training, the factors would be found in an analysis of the company's objectives, present performance of managerial personnel, areas of deficiencies, and the overall quality of the management human resources under consideration.

A cost-reduction objective would involve analysis of actual present and projected costs, the "reason-whys" for these costs, areas where the opportunities for cost reduction exist, and what is known about present methods and procedures.

A problem involving production would have to delve into the existing facts about the actual production operations, the repertoire of the worker skills involved, available equipment, plant layout, together with what would be needed for a more desirable situation.

Selling your idea. To increase *your* chances of success in presenting ideas, here are several time-tested guidelines.

The value of understatement. Avoid hard sell. New ideas cannot be rammed through with mere exuberant rhetoric. They require subtle, fact-buttressed persuasion. Enthusiasm can be profitably contagious, but a superabundance of it—especially in the beginning of the presentation, when the full story still has to unfold—will put people on the defensive right from the beginning.

Tell what's behind your idea. Before the actual presentation of the idea, give a short background history of the problem, what led you to investigate the area, and how you proceeded to solve the problem.

Get to the point—clearly. Make your presentation as concise and to-the-point as possible. People become impatient with long-winded preliminaries and side issues. Avoid jargon or technical language unless the people you are addressing are at home with it. It's a very human tendency to distrust what one does not understand.

Two main parts. Have your presentation include a broad, overall consideration of the idea—and the problem it is designed to solve—then follow up with a detailed discussion covering execution and implementation.

Illustrate your points. A light touch helps. The most direct way is through easy-to-see illustrations, pictures, drawings, photos, models, sketches, diagrams, charts, or a blackboard. Purely oral demonstrations are more quickly forgotten.

Don't use unsubstantiated claims. Many sound ideas are turned down because irrelevant arguments and/or unsubstantiated evidence are used to support them. Have a complete dossier of supportive facts and figures at your fingertips.

Try omitting a vital detail. When it's picked up by one of the listeners and added at his suggestion, you suddenly have two proponents for your idea.

Introduce counterarguments. A two-sided approach in which you give arguments for and against will help convince the more sophisticated of your thoroughness. It also takes the wind out of objections or reservations toward the project.

Don't fret over anticipated questions. Worry could spoil your presentation. On the other hand, be prepared to answer all possible questions, and give all the facts about the idea.

Avoid an argumentative approach. The person who goes into a presentation with the conviction that people are going to resist any ideas he presents is likely to find them responding just the way he thinks they will.

Two ways of neutralizing objections. Ask a series of questions with which the person who objects has to agree. Posing skillful questions also crystallizes the thinking of everyone present.

Or just listen to the objections calmly and thoughtfully, encouraging the person who objects to expand and elaborate. Not being as familiar with the idea as you are, he will soon exhaust his objections as well as run out of answers to your own counterpoints.

Welcome suggestions for revision. Try not to reject revisions—they may even improve your idea. Welcome them, for the person making the revision has taken an interest and now has a personal stake in your idea. There is always room to share credit with others on ideas.

If at all possible, make others feel they are participants, "co-creators" of your idea, rather than passive listeners who must sit in judgment. The "we approach" rather than the "I approach" has been the single most important ingredient in many successful idea-selling situations.

Be natural. While your manner should be confident and poised, never assume an air of superiority when presenting your idea.

Benjamin Franklin realized the wisdom of natural presentation when he said, "The way to sell an idea to another is to state your case moderately and accurately. This causes your listener to be receptive and, like as not, he will turn about and convince you of the worth of your idea. But if you go at him in a tone of positiveness and arrogance, you are likely to turn him against your idea, no matter how good it is."

Map out the steps to be taken. Suggest easy actions to take, or offer to test the idea if this can be done with relative ease.

Break off and wrap up. After the presentation, arrange for a break and discussion period. Give participants a chance to sort through the material and their impressions. Then field the questions as thoroughly and thoughtfully as possible. Sum up the idea's more salient points, its anticipated benefits and advantages, and emphasize its necessity. Remember, sound ideas deserve salable presentations.

#70: PINE CONE: SENSORY-AWARENESS ENHANCEMENT

Sensory awareness is not an outright gift. However, it can be developed by constantly using your senses in responding to your environment. Your experiences with the cone were just the beginning. Make sensory involvement a continuous process of exploration and discovery. Whenever you have a few unoccupied moments, pick up any object that is around you—a fallen leaf, a flower, a coin—and explore its sensuous characteristics. In each situation prolong the search and enjoy the pleasures.

#71: KICK THAT BLOCK

Examples
Fear of failure
Fear of making a mistake or of criticism
Tendency to prematurely judge ideas
Need to conform
Intolerance of ambiguity
Inability to perceive what the real problem is
Lack of frustration-tolerance
Using wrong approaches to solve problems
Insistence on being logical
Distrust of intuitive thinking
Inability to utilize all one's abilities
Laziness
Pathological desire for security
Lack of endurance and perseverance
Lack of inner quietude
Jumping to conclusions
Smugnosis
Disinterest, indifference, lack of desire to create
Belief that indulging in fantasy is useless
Lack of curiosity
Faulty observation and insensitivity to clues
Superficiality, shallowness, incompleteness, and hastiness of thought
Difficulty in seeing remote relationships
Inhibited inquisitiveness
Lack of knowledge of one's field
Fear of making a fool of oneself
Lack of flexibility
Overmotivation to succeed
Being overwhelmed by the immensity of a problem
Incorrect problem statement
Tendency to cling to habitual, routine ways of thinking
Concrete or practical mindedness
Fear of being a pioneer
Fear of being too aggressive

#72: MAKE A "BUG LIST"

Examples
   Poor TV programs
   Windowshades that won't go down or up
   Telephone ringing and no one answers
   Paperless toilets
   Drippy faucets
   Defective mirrors
   Dusty furniture
   Roaches in food
   Burnt toast
   Electric fixtures interfering with TV
   Dull knives
   Pets that aren't housebroken
   Cleaning Kitty Litter
   Overripe bananas
   Broken shoelaces
   Dog droppings on lawn
   Drawers that stick
   Car horns
   Cigar smoke
   Wobbly chairs
   Crowded beaches

#73: CREATIVE DAYDREAMING

Until recently, daydreaming or fantasy making was considered either a waste of time or a symptom of maladjustment. Most psychologists branded habitual daydreaming as evidence of neurotic tendencies or as an escape from the responsibilities of the everyday world. They warned that habitual daydreaming would eventually alienate a person from society and reduce his or her effectiveness in coping with real-life problems. Even those behavioral scientists who were more indulgent considered daydreaming "a sublimated drive gratification" or a "compensatory substitute" for the real things in life. The most prevalent stereotype of a daydreamer pictured him as a person lost in fantasies, busily weaving images of heroic Walter Mitty achievements, travel to distant never-never lands, or romantic conquests and sexual fulfillment.

As with anything carried to excess, daydreaming can be harmful. There are those who almost completely substitute a fantasy life for the rewards of activity in the real world. And when the fantasy addict withdraws from reality, his or her psychological health is impaired.

But these situations are very rare indeed. The truth is that most people suffer from a *lack* of fantasy making, rather than an *excess* of it. We now know how valuable creative daydreaming really is. There is a growing realization that if we were completely prevented from daydreaming, our emotional balance would be rendered precarious. Not only would we be less able to deal with the pressures of day-to-day existence, but self-control and self-direction would be in danger of being relinquished.

Daydreaming Is Your Safety Valve. Prolonged daydream deprivation results in mounting anxiety and tension. In fact, when the need to daydream can no longer be suppressed, daydreaming erupts spontaneously.

During times of stress, daydreaming erects for our nervous system a temporary shelter to shield us from the icy winds of reality, much in the same way that building a house protects our bodies from the elements. Both may be seen as forms of escapism, but no sane man or woman wants to spend his or her life in an unrelieved battle for survival. Surely we are entitled to occasional strategic withdrawals to regroup our forces.

Some Recent Findings. Recent research on daydreaming indicates that it is an intrinsic part of daily life and that a certain amount of daydreaming each day is essential for relaxation.

But the beneficial effects of daydreaming go beyond relaxation and the reduction of tension. According to experiments conducted by Dr. Joan T. Freyberg, a New York City-based psychotherapist, daydreaming significantly helps learning ability, powers of concentration, attention span, and the ability to interact and communicate with others. She also discovered that those of her patients who easily engage in fantasy making usually respond more quickly to treatment and are better able to cope with frustrations and crises.

In an experiment with schoolchildren, Dr. Freyberg observed that daydreaming improved their concentration: "There was less running around, more happy feelings, more talking and playing with each other, and more attention to detail." It has also been found that those children who daydream regularly are least likely to develop crippling emotional disorders.

In still another experiment, psychologist Dr. Sara Similansky discovered that the men and women who were taught how to daydream significantly improved their language and other skills. And Dr. Jerome L. Singer, at Yale University, found that daydreaming resulted in improved self-control and enhanced creative thinking. Dr. Singer also points out that daydreaming is a way to improve upon reality and that it helps a person to cope with delay, frustration, and deprivation. It frequently helps us to change difficult situations into more manageable ones and it gives impetus to meaningful future planning. Daydreaming gives us greater strength and resolve to overcome the obstacles and difficulties as we move toward our objectives, and it is a powerful spur to achievement.

Other clinical and experimental research has indicated that daydreaming helps us to better understand our own behavior and to achieve a more intimate rapport with, and acceptance of, our inner feelings. This in turn helps us to relate better to other people.

We have traveled far in a relatively short time span: from considering daydreaming as trival or pathological self-absorption, to the present view that it is an important human skill for the enrichment of life, available to anyone who wants to practice it. Several psychotherapeutic techniques, among them Guided Affective Imagery, Behaviorist Desensitization, Psychosynthesis, and Programmed Visualization, make use of deliberate daydreaming and fantasy making.

Daydreaming Can Solve Your Problems. It has been found that daydreaming improves a person's ability to be better attuned to practical, immediate concerns, to solve everyday problems, make decisions, and come up with new ideas more readily. Contrary to popular belief, incessant and conscious effort at solving a problem is in reality one of the most inefficient ways of tackling it. While initial effort is necessary when we face a problem, it has been discovered that an effective solution to an especially difficult or bothersome situation frequently occurs when conscious attempts to solve it have been suspended. Answers to intractable problems that seem to come from "out of the blue" are invariably due to daydreaming about your problem in a relaxed way. This is because daydreaming enables you to break out of the tyranny of your intellect into the freedom of your intuition.

Daydreaming Helps in Self-Discovery. Daydreaming does not have to pursue the impossible, the will-o'-the-wisp. On the contrary, for many people a passive retreat into the private world of reverie is their "royal road" to making their reality more meaningful. Daydreaming helps them in self-discovery, in finding out who they are and what they really would want to do. They use daydreaming as "a blind date with their deeper selves," as a means for canvassing alternatives, for discovering fresh directions to serve as a compass in their future actions. They use it for taking stock of their values, desires, annoyances, wishes, fears, and plans for the future.

Even our best-laid plans and objectives frequently change or become lost behind the haze and hurry of practical concerns. Daydreaming helps us to repel as foreign matter the excess baggage of irrelevant concerns that frequently block action on our more fundamental goals. It helps us to put our true concerns, the things that are really relevant to us, into sharper focus. And in this way we can actually improve the quality of our lives.

Daydreaming and the Attainment of Success. Many successful men and women actually daydream their future successes and achievements. Daydreaming for them bears a direct relationship to its expression in overt behavior.

In sports, for example, John Uelses, former pole-vaulting champion, made use of deliberate, programmed daydreaming. Before each meet he vividly pictured himself clearing the bar at a certain height. He repeatedly visualized not only all the minute details of the "act of winning," but actually "saw" the stadium, the crowds present, and even "smelled" the grass and the earth. The resulting "memory traces" influenced his actual performance during the meet toward the vividly pictured goal of success.

Jack Nicklaus daydreams before each tournament to attain what he calls "the winning feeling." This feeling, as he puts it, "gives me a line to the cup just as clearly as if it's been tattooed on my brain. With that feeling all I have to do is swing the clubs and let nature take its course."

Jim Thorpe utilized strong mental imagery to picture success before each sporting event. Author Lew Miller relates this story about him. "Once he was on a ship headed for the Olympics. Other stars were running around the deck or exercising vigorously. The track coach spotted Thorpe, his decathlon entrant, sitting propped against a cabin with his eyes closed. 'What do you think you're doing?' the coach demanded. 'Just practicing,' replied Jim. He then explained that while relaxing he was seeing himself successfully competing in his specialty. History has recorded his legendary feats and record-breaking performances. Jim Thorpe knew instinctively how mental images work."

Vivid Daydreams Improve the Self-Image. Why would a vivid projection of success help to bring the success about? "Your nervous system cannot tell the difference between an *imagined* experience and a *real* experience," says surgeon and author Dr. Maxwell Maltz. "In either case, it reacts automatically to information which you give to it from your forebrain. Your nervous system reacts appropriately to what you think or imagine to be true." He further maintains that the exercise of daydreaming "builds new 'memories' or stored data into your midbrain and central nervous system." These positive memories in turn improve self-image, and this has a telling impact on a person's behavior and accomplishments.

A life lived without fantasy and daydream is a seriously impoverished life. Each of us should put aside a few minutes each day and daydream, sort of take a ten or fifteen minute vacation. It is highly beneficial to your physical and mental well-being, and you will find that this modest investment in time will add up to a more creative and imaginative, a more satisfied and a more self-fulfilled you, in a relatively short time. The art of successful daydreaming offers a fuller sense of being intensely alive from moment to moment, and this of course contributes greatly to excitement and zest in living.

#74: IMAGINE!

Examples
   I. If you think you have no problems, create some.
      Ideas make the world go around.

Imagination will find a way.

Intelligent people are not always creative.

M. Most people are more creative than they think they are.

Many problems are not solved because we give up quickly.

Make creativity a habit.

Minds need exercise just as our bodies do.

A. An idea is only as good as the use you put it to.

Attack problems wholeheartedly.

Achievement requires more effort than creativity.

Adventurous-spirited minds are more creative.

G. Generate a new idea every day.

Giving up before you solve a problem is for losers.

Grandfather was always right—seventy years ago.

Good ideas come when you're having fun.

I. In creativity you have to do what feels right.

Is a creative person made or born?

Ideas that appear far-out today may be old hat tomorrow.

Ideas are only as good as the use they're put to.

N. No one knows how creative a person really is.

New ideas can be used to fight bad habits.

No one is always in peak form—relaxation can be creative too.

Never mind what others think—use your own judgment.

New ways of doing things are not always the best.

E. Everything is interesting if you want it to be.

Exchange thoughts with others—this will spark new ideas.

Enthusiasm helps a person to become more creative.

Express your ideas—if you don't, others will.

#75: THE ULTIMATE

Answer: The words THE END upside down.

If the words did not pop into view at first glance, you would have recognized what these incomplete lines represent if you had done some filling in.

Creative people have the ability to bring up incomplete or unclear patterns from memory storage and make them complete. They need, as a rule, only a few clues to identify something.

PART III

A New Look at the Creative Process

ONE OF THE MOST persistent notions about creative ideas is that they come with flashlike spontaneity. Composer Paul Hindemith described how such a conception occurs: "We all know the impression of a very heavy flash of lightning in the night. Within a second's time, we see a broad landscape, not only in its general outline but with every detail. . . . Compositions must be conceived in the same way. If we cannot, in the flash of a single moment, see a composition in its absolute entirety with every pertinent detail in its proper place, we are not genuine creators."

Although some creative ideas do owe their existence to such spontaneous insight, closer study of the creative process indicates that most novel concepts do not come forth full-blown and precisely delineated. Nor does the subsequent process of forming and developing an idea always flow spontaneously from the unconscious, thereby reducing the creative person to the role of a passive transcriber of dictated ideas.

The dramatic, sudden illumination that would enable the creative person to perceive a novel idea in its entirety is in reality a rare but overpublicized phenomenon.

You are more creative than you think

Unfortunately, this romantic notion of complete vision has become firmly rooted among contemporary investigators of, and writers on, creativity. Its perpetuation only serves to convince those who have failed to experience such inspired visions that they really do not have creative talent, when, in fact, they may possess it to a considerable degree. This notion has dissuaded many promising creative men and women from wholeheartedly applying their talents.

Scrutiny shows that what does occur during the creative process is a slow, selective construction of an idea that is at first only imperfectly grasped, and that follows the dictates of intuition as to what does and does not belong, what is and what is not proper.

Imagine yourself standing on a shore on a foggy day. A ship

sailing in the distance is enshrouded by fog. You alternately catch a glimpse of part of its sail, the top of its mast, its prow. Although you never get a full view, you know the ship is there, and you eventually do construct an image of it in its entirety.

Similarly, at the beginning of the creative process you sense the total structure of your idea even though you have perceived only a limited number of its details. You start elaborating on these few details, and this process of elaboration and shaping helps other details to emerge. If you withhold critical judgment, these additional details often fall into place spontaneously.

Thus, the initial idea—rather than being comprehensive of the whole conception—is often only a fragment of what is still to emerge.

Although this is so, the total idea nevertheless controls the entire creative process—so much so in fact that it is impossible for the creative person to put elements into the evolving idea that do not fit its predominant configuration. Intuitive sensing, therefore (and not an all-embracing insight), serves as the vital measure of which elements are to be incorporated into the creation.

William J. J. Gordon, of Synectics, Inc., observed this process of intuition in his invention-design group: "Intuition is an inner judgment made by the individual about a concept relative to a problem on which he is working. . . . The individual with good intuition is the one who, beyond what could be expected from mere probability alone, repeatedly selects the viewpoint which turns out to lead, for instance, to a great painting or an important invention."

In a vital sense, the creative process can be considered as movement: from the amorphous, dimly perceived idea toward an intelligible structure; from obscure inwardness toward tangible clarity; from the implicit toward the explicit; from the chaotic toward the organized.

Creativity depends on suspending judgment

Nothing inhibits the creative process more than critical judgment of an emerging idea. On this there is unanimous agreement among creative persons and investigators of creativity. One must resist the mounting pressure to criticize the progressively articulated portions of an idea.

One of the primary reasons why judiciousness and creativity make uncomfortable bedfellows is that criticism is based on what has already been accepted. Critical judgment must have recourse to precedent and facts—everything that is past.

This being so, judgment is essentially opposed to the untried, the original. For creative advancement, the past serves as a guidepost only to a limited degree. By itself, however, judgment is incapable of either bringing forth a new idea or of predicting what would happen if it were developed.

The knowledge of what already exists also involves stereotyped orientation. None of the unexpectedly new combinations of elements in a creative idea, in its formative stage, meet the requirements of established facts or logic. A new idea is of course based on available knowledge, but it does not issue from it by any direct rational process.

Failure to suspend judgment and consider a range of alternatives frequently results in early commitment to an approach that may contain a "restrictive error" or an "incorrigible strategy." For example, subjects in a perceptual laboratory who made an early, incorrect interpretation of a picture on an "ambigu-meter" (a device that gradually brings a blurred picture into focus) tended to retain the wrong perception. They failed to "see" even after the picture had been fully and clearly exposed.

This does not mean that critical judgment has no place in the production of a new idea. On the contrary, it serves a useful purpose—but only at the end of the process, when an objective assessment of the idea should be attempted.

Critical attitude destroys creativity in others

That critical and evaluative attitudes can stifle creativity in others has been noted by many researchers. As psychologist A. R. Wight points out: "A person will submit ideas with increasing reluctance if these are pounced upon immediately and subjected to critical and often merciless evaluation. It is difficult for a new idea to survive this kind of treatment. The effect on the individual suggesting the idea is equally devastating. Attacking his idea is felt to be, and often is, an attack on him personally. The individual feels hostility toward and often loses respect for the person initiating the attack.

He soon refrains from suggesting anything at all. Or he resorts to second-guessing in an attempt to suggest something that will be accepted and approved."

One way to lessen the harmful effects of criticism is by learning to be tactful when we have to criticize. We should be receptive to ideas and suggestions by becoming understanding listeners. We should learn to evaluate ideas without resorting to external evaluation—that is, we should *react* to ideas rather than *judge* them.

The ability to remain coolly objective in the face of criticism comes only with time. It is founded on successes in creative problem-solving. No matter how tough the individual, ridicule, criticism, or even indifference by others to his ideas can destroy his creativity.

The emotional concomitants

Among the observable characteristics of an emerging new idea is the sharp sense of value attached to it. It arrives brimming with positiveness, giving the creative thinker a sense of certainty about its relevance to the problem.

This positiveness that infuses the idea undoubtedly lies at the root of many great achievements; still, it is not everything, for the difficult process of shaping it into something workable lies ahead.

The idea alone is too often believed to be all there is to the creative process. Yet almost everyone has known of idea men who could figuratively shake ideas from their sleeves, but who rarely accomplished much because they failed to work their ideas out into something practical.

Nevertheless, for most creative men and women the conviction as to the importance of their idea, and the exaltation it instills in them, are largely the reason for starting the creative process. Additionally, this positive feeling provides the creative person with the staying power to conquer every deficiency or temporary blockage that may occur, and drives him or her to understand the idea in its smallest detail.

The intuitive moment is also frequently accompanied by a sense of compulsion that drives the creative person to do something immediately with the idea. It recurrently invades his consciousness, charging his thoughts to further develop the idea. This compulsion may even obstruct the emergence of other ideas if it is not satisfied.

How to handle ideas

Creative ideas are often notoriously evanescent and elusive. At the moment when the idea appears, the person feels that it would be impossible to forget it. Yet, only moments later, the impression becomes blurred or fades away altogether. If the creative individual fails to capture ideas when they occur, fails to fix them in some form for later reference, they vanish and seldom return.

There are creative individuals, however, who prefer not to make a notation of their ideas until they become more fully structured. They allow glimmerings of an idea to occur to them a number of times without committing them to daylight. The reason for this is that some ideas take time to mature, and with each successive emergence of them into consciousness, they become more firmly developed.

It is imperative, however, that novice creators fix the unexpected ideas in some form as soon as they emerge. As we all have experienced time and again, some ideas appear to us brimming with important meaning at the time of their intrusion into consciousness, yet a later recall of them often fails to occur.

An accomplished creative person learns from long practice and frequent disappointments the proper technique for handling ideas. He learns, for example, that some ideas should be jotted down immediately, as soon as they occur, while others should be kept fluid and outside conscious focus until the last possible instant. Still others should be dropped back into the unconscious for further development and incubation.

As a general rule, the more complex the idea, the more advisable it is to postpone a commitment to paper. Otherwise there is the real danger of forcing the original implicit idea irretrievably into a restrictive scheme, the limitations of which can straitjacket any subsequent development.

In the final analysis, the dilemma of whether to immediately capture or to incubate an idea has to be solved by each individual alone. A prevalent notion among many investigators of creativity seems to be that initial ideas—those that occur when a person is first faced with finding a solution to a problem—are valueless. This may be true when the problem is relatively unfamiliar and when conscious effort has not been previously spent on it. However, when a problem has been through a period of unconscious cerebration, the first ideas that follow are frequently the best. Consequently, it is advisable to pay closer attention to the first ideas that occur during a productive mood even though the effortless fashion in which they often appear may make them suspect.

The primacy of the whole

The creative process begins with the *intuitive moment*. This is when the creative individual first grasps the overall essence of an idea that might solve the problem. This intimation of the wholeness of the idea comes into being during the creative process through the channel of feeling or intuition. This intuition also directs the shaping of the idea's details during its progressive articulation.

This intimation of the whole has to persevere through every phase of the progressive molding of the idea, until the person finally feels that he can give his approval to the outcome. A sense of completion accompanies this act, which signifies that the original concept has been more or less fully exploited.

The original overall grasp of the idea furnishes both the end and the means for achieving the end. It guides the elaboration of the idea safely through the shifting chaos of an enormous number of either unconsciously or consciously perceived alternatives and details, to its unique terminus. The intimation of an idea's totality controls its details: rejecting some possibilities, accepting others, molding the latter into the elements of the final outcome.

It occasionally happens that many of the elements and details that are first incorporated into a creation may later be dropped, when seen to be irrelevant, and others may take their place. But this does not argue against the theory that it is the implicit whole that determines what is and what is not admitted into the evolving idea. Only when the individual has firmly grasped the intimated whole can he burrow to the appropriate data in his memory and assemble the elements that contribute toward the development of the idea. Only then can he properly elaborate the idea, selecting from past observations, restructuring, combining, and transforming the details. The criterion for this process of elaboration remains the immediate feeling of whether or not particular details do or do not contribute to the emerging configuration. This intuitive feeling continues until the moment when the person finds that he cannot add or change anything about his product to improve it.

Distractions impair creativity

One chief reason why the creative process almost invariably produces a strain is because the intimation of the implicit idea and its developmental direction must be maintained at all costs—throughout unwelcome distractions (whether external or internal), momentary inhibitions, periods of fatigue or flagging interest, times of doubt about the idea's value, and remembered other obligations and concerns that make up the creative individual's environment.

Of course, the process of creation occurs quite differently when a person can become totally absorbed in the task. He then attends to the work unhampered by the strain of having to sift an excess of consciously perceived alternatives at each successive step in the idea's development. He does whatever his unconscious promptings lead him to do, and ultimately finds that his idea has grown effortlessly and spontaneously.

As a rule, ideas developed in this fashion need very little revision. However, this mode of creating, although coveted, occurs rarely or cannot be maintained for too long a period. Constraint, mounting effort, and tension inevitably set in.

As tension mounts beyond an optimum point, the creative individual senses that he is being forced to spend more effort for less results, finds that errors start to pile up, and that his direction becomes rambling and confused.

This is when most creative people quit. More obstinate ones may stick to their work, taking recourse to their richly stocked bag of past methods or continuing to consciously elaborate as much as possible in tune with the initial concept.

Numerous rough drafts attest however that it is almost impossible for the creative individual to consciously assume conformity with the intimated end of his new idea when the hum of the mood has stopped and when he finds himself no longer tuned in to the unconscious. The firmer his anticipation of the initial totality, the easier it is for him to shape its emerging derivatives, ward off adventitious conscious choices, and arrive at a satisfactory creative product.

The end is also the means

Many scientists have noted that an intuitive moment indicates the arrival of a possible solution. Albert Einstein, for example, is said to have had the capacity to feel the direction of a possible solution for his problem before he actually knew what the solution was. He always trusted and acted upon his hunches.

When a person starts to research a particular problem, he is usually already under the sway of an intuitive hunch that imputes relevance to the facts he so assiduously collects. No person ever has a hunch, nor can he pose a problem, if he is wholly in the dark about a possible solution and what data he needs to arrive at a solution. If he does not arrive at a satisfactory explanation, the trouble may lie in the complexity of the problem, but seldom in the genuineness of the original hunch.

Selectivity in the creative process

The best evidence that there is an intimation of an implicit wholeness at the intuitive moment is the highly selective activity that occurs throughout the creative process. Selectivity works through the intuitive feeling of moment-to-moment appropriateness of the details and elements being incorporated into the evolving idea, guiding their choice and the way they are to be used.

Selectivity operates during the total spectrum of the creative endeavor, starting with the choice of the problem to be undertaken. In addition to the compelling preference exhibited toward a problem, there is the selection of specific data to be collected to form the groundwork for solving the problem and developing an idea. During the process of developing the idea itself, selectivity operates to admit elements and details that belong and to suppress those that do not. Thus, selectivity cuts across all the facets of the creative process.

In the beginning stages, the structure of intimated wholeness is only vaguely felt. Many of the details, their balances and correspondences, although tending toward the implicit wholeness, are not quite consistent or congruent with it. Consequently, much restructuring is necessary before the requirements of the implicit configuration are satisfied. But so pervasive and insistent is the established sense of the idea's whole, so unifying is its pull, that it imposes the conditions for its realization and inexorably demands the proper transformations and rearrangements.

Conditions that contribute to creativity

The appearance of new ideas cannot easily be foretold (except, possibly, a feeling of peculiar restlessness just before the advent of one), and it is quite impossible to induce ideas at will. Creative ideas are not under our voluntary control, and as a consequence cannot be governed by planning, schedules, or sheer enforcement.

But once the creative current is running strongly and the organic development of the idea is under way, one can assume an attitude that resembles will and that does help to maintain creativity at a desirable intensity. This may be a wish, a challenging urge on the part of the creative individual to give his or her utmost while submitting to the creative act.

A genuinely creative person desires to transcend his past performance, to give his best on every new occasion of problem solving, and thus achieve more than was aspired to before. This urgent wish toward fuller self-realization helps the creative individual to sustain the intensity of the creative mood and to keep the avenues of the unconscious free from both internal and external interruptions, as well as from the habit patterns of consciousness.

Choose your best time for creating

Although it is impossible to induce creative ideas at will, there are nevertheless certain conditions that are propitious for the evocation of ideas. For example, for many people the night is most conducive to the creative mood. This is the time when many creative individuals begin (as one person put it) "a blind date with their deeper selves." Night, with its pervading peacefulness and mystery, brings to them a sense of isolation conducive to creation.

Daytime, on the other hand, with its predominantly practical orientation, its bustle and noise, can block creativity and prevent the flow from the unconscious.

There are of course people who prefer the early-morning hours, the freshness of a newly born day.

Again, others need high-powered activity around them in order to find release for their ideas. They have to be in the whirlwind of restless activity to receive the stimulus. Many such men and women have the knack of closing out the external world at will, of being able to detach themselves whenever necessary to set ideas into motion.

Many creative individuals can tune in to their private selves in the noisiest of environments. The condition of inward isolation, however, is a primary requirement for significant creative work. Indeed, such moments of detachment from one's external environment can be more productive than hours of merely physical isolation.

The power of eccentric rituals

Many of the apparently trivial idiosyncrasies of creative men and women that provide entertaining anecdotes for biographers actually helped to evoke and then to sustain the creative mood.

Debussy often gazed at the Seine and the reflections of the setting sun on its waves to establish an atmosphere for composing. Schiller kept rotten apples in his desk drawer because their aroma helped him to evoke a creative mood. Dostoevsky found that he could best dream up stories and characters while doodling.

It seems that there is hardly a creative individual who does not have a ritual, an eccentricity for provoking free-floating concentration and an uncensored alertness to the implications of an idea.

Such idiosyncrasies seem also necessary for keeping the overactive thought-patterns of consciousness in abeyance, and for shutting out all distractions. Anchoring oneself so singly mutes outward distractions. This is essential, for the shrill ringing of the telephone in a neighboring room, a conversation down the hall, a rumbling noise in the distance, even momentary bodily discomfitures, can shatter the protective bubble of the creative mood. By channeling one's attention into a ritual, all distractions lose their power to disrupt.

Many creative individuals pace the floor endlessly, and biographies are replete with instances of ideas occurring to creative individuals when they were walking or traveling. That physical motion animates and augments the imagination; that our legs are the wheels of thought, has long been known.

Many creative workers frequently claim that the ideas they value most occur to them during passive, relaxed, or even fatigued states of half-waking. It is well known that Newton solved many of his problems when his attention was waylaid by complete relaxation. Similarly, Edison knew the value of half-waking states, and, whenever confronted with a seemingly insurmountable barrier that defied all his efforts, he would stretch out on a couch in his workshop—brought there for just this reason—and try to fall asleep.

Insignificant incidents may stimulate

The creative mood may seize an individual without any detectable reason or stimulus. It apparently can be catalyzed by insignificant and wayward incidents. Because intuitive moments cannot be voluntarily controlled, creative ideas may, and do, appear at any hour and under the strangest of circumstances.

For example, there is a story about Vivaldi being overcome by inspiration while celebrating Mass. As soon as the "divine afflatus" had struck him, he rushed away from the altar into the sacristy, where he wrote down his theme. It was only after he had carefully marked down the melody and assured himself of its retention that he returned to the altar to resume the Mass. Needless to say, the officials of the church, ignorant of the waywardness of the creative process, summarily dismissed him from his office.

An incident that has been reported about Newton was that, during the course of a dinner for guests, he left the table to get some wine from the cellar. On his way, he was overcome by an idea, forgot his errand and company, and was soon hard at work in his study.

Many seasoned creative individuals have an unreasoned, intuitive sense for such preparatory cues and the external conditions necessary for evoking a creative mood. Although it is impossible to summon creative ideas at will, many such men and women have mastered the trick of exposing themselves to stimuli that make the occurrence of the creative mood possible. Experience eventually shows every creative person which conditions are personally propitious.

There are of course long stretches of barren periods in every creative individual's life. There are periods when the incipient mood for productive activity serves only to arouse conflicts instead of ideas, with the result that people may lapse into a state of lassitude in which excuses are found to postpone creative work, sometimes for months or years.

The creative person should establish regular habits of work. He should regulate and coordinate the acquisition of fresh information and impressions, allow time for their digestion and the incubation of ideas, and note how long it takes for an insight to emerge and to elaborate it into reality. He is likely to be most creative when adhering to his individual rhythm for these phases. Violations of this rhythm because of undue haste, or even of tardiness, can retard creative efficiency.